Simplicity

1834

Also by Jon Howard Hall

Noccalula: Cherokee Princess of Alabama
A Short Story (available only as an eBook)

Kyzer's Destiny

Kyzer's Promise

Corporal Archer and the Siege of Vicksburg

A Place Called Winston

Simplicity

1834

A Novel of Historical Fiction

JON HOWARD HALL

SIMPLICITY 1834
A NOVEL OF HISTORICAL FICTION

iUniverse books may be ordered through booksellers or by contacting:

iUniverse
1663 Liberty Drive
Bloomington, IN 47403
www.iuniverse.com
844-349-9409

ISBN: 978-1-6632-5251-7 (sc)
ISBN: 978-1-6632-5253-1 (hc)
ISBN: 978-1-6632-5252-4 (e)

Library of Congress Control Number: 2023908078

Print information available on the last page.

iUniverse rev. date: 08/16/2023

For all my friends in
Marion, Alabama

Contents

Prologue

Simplicity ...
Why that particular name?

I really don't have a clue, but when I look at the root words, I see *simple* and *city*. Perhaps a realistic meaning would be called "a simple place in the city." Maybe in due time, I will discover how the name actually came into existence. However, I can speculate since I seem to be good at that sometimes.

For instance, it could have been at some point, the Perry County Historical Society decided to re-name the old Huntington-Locke house while they began to call it *Simplicity*. Rather than that, maybe the name was derived from the actual physical appearance of the little house itself. Regardless, Simplicity is known to be structured in the style of a Greek Revival cottage that was built in 1834. It is located in the Western Historical District in Marion, Alabama, which is known today as the College City, est. 1817.

Before I continue, I should probably stop here to explain the reason for my particular interest in Simplicity. That's really simple in itself and quite easy to explain.

I have always had a keen interest in old historic places and houses, especially the architecture during the period 1840-1865. Along with that, a dream to actually own a "grand old place" someday was always on my mind. That dream came true for me on October 31, 2019, when I closed the "no brainer" deal of a lifetime to purchase and make Simplicity my own. What a great feeling, just let me tell you!

Not giving up, I had been looking nearly thirty years at vintage antebellum and Victorian homes, particularly in Georgia and Alabama. One of my favorite places for many years of searching kept leading me to a Greek Revival plantation home built in 1861 and located on famous South Lee Street in Americus, Georgia. A couple of years ago, when Liberty Hall first appeared on the market, I was quite disappointed to find the listing price was completely out of my range. I dearly loved that old place, and I always considered it to be my ultimate dream home at the time, but it was not to be, I guess.

Much earlier than that, I was getting quite serious over a grand old Victorian in Plains, Georgia, with beautiful heart pine floors and glass doorknobs. I remember almost quitting my job in Birmingham to relocate in Plains, get a job there or somewhere in south Georgia, and buy the place that was built next door to the Plains First Baptist Church (attended at one time by former President Jimmy Carter). Needless to say, that deal fell through and never happened. Following that time, as the years passed, I began to look once more and think about several places in south Alabama. The Black Belt region seemed rich in affordable properties located in Eufaula, Montgomery, Selma, Greensboro, and Marion. I finally set my sight in that direction while beginning to concentrate down in the southwest county of Perry in the lovely little town of Marion.

The search began online while I would occasionally find myself clicking on the Historic Icon on the Bill Mackey Real Estate webpage at this time. It was probably twelve or thirteen years ago when I first made an appointment with an agent to actually see this particular home which was located almost to the end of West Lafayette Street. I remember that I really liked the place very much, but at the time, felt it needed so much work and TLC that I chose not to purchase. No regrets, so I just kept looking and waiting for the best deal to appear at some future time, and as always, wishing and hoping for a new discovery at the right time and place.

Guess what? That finally happened on October 1, 2019, when I saw this same house for a second time to take another look after all these years. I found so many things had been upgraded, and after the initial walk-through, I was convinced that it felt so much like the place I had always imagined. I finally found my dream home!

Do I live there? Yes and no. It is a second home for me and my wife since our major residence remains in St. Clair County. My plan is to make Simplicity my personal retreat, a place where I can come to be alone while I continue to write and enjoy a change of scene. We are hoping to continue to restore and furnish most of the rooms with period furniture from the 1850's while repainting the plaster walls with colors that were used also during that time.

Marion is truly a great place to live, so friendly, and it

is especially nice to have already met so many unique and wonderful friends.

I would have to say for myself, the best part of the house, other than the general layout and grounds, is the actual history. When I discovered who built the house and the family who first lived there, I was so intrigued that I had to learn more about them. It was actually my real estate agent who recommended a book about that particular family that set my wheels spinning. I'm thinking now about a great subject for my next book perhaps, so I plan to write it as a historical fiction. Persons that were real will be described using their given names as such, but others may be composites or simply drawn from my own imagination while they become a part of the story. Certain true events that happened will always be described as accurate as possible, while other fictional events may be included as I may choose to add to the drama of that particular scene.

This is for real ...

Someone has asked me already, "Seen or heard any ghosts in the house?"

Well ... maybe just one, so far. I will try to explain as best I can what I experienced during the early morning hours on February 22, 2020.

The temperature outside was in the 40's that night, and I had the thermostat set to 72 degrees as I settled into bed. The gas heat would kick on and off which was normal, and I was used to the sound it made when this would happen. I am alone in the house. I was asleep in the small bedroom on the back of the house. The headboard of my bed is located on the wall it shared with the back wall of the parlor. In other words, located on the other side of the bedroom is the room I have designated as the parlor. When I first took possession of the house, the parlor room floor had been completely covered with wood paneling, not flooring. I had all the paneling removed to discover three small areas of damage to the original heart pine floor. Pieces of scrap paneling had been placed over the open holes in the floor in order to keep out the cold and any critters who could easily come up from the crawlspace. A few pieces of small items and boxes were placed along the back wall, and other than that, the room was quite bare and the parlor door was always kept closed.

So, at exactly 1:59 a.m. I am awakened as I look at the clock on my nightstand. I sit straight up in bed to listen to the noise which stopped a few seconds later when the clock showed 2:00 a.m. That took less than a minute while I sat there on the side of the bed for the next five minutes thinking about what just happened in there. Feeling dazed, I never went to look, so I lay back down to go back to sleep. Was this a dream? I don't think so. Was it maybe a cat, a rat, a possum underneath the floor? Who knows? Was it the heat kicking on? I don't believe so. What was it then? Here it is:

I heard actual footsteps which sounded like a man in boots slowly walking across the floor in the parlor.

All I can say is that if I had heard that parlor door open, I was reaching for my pistol. I don't really believe in ghosts or spirits, but now, I am more aware of any strange things that could possibly happen in my house built in 1834.

The first thing in the morning, I went straight to the

parlor door and opened it. I couldn't see anything that had moved, fallen, or was out of place anywhere in the room. As for me and what I felt at the time, I had no plans for an exorcist, but if something else ever happens here, I will be calling Ghostbusters!

That's all well and good, but I'm thinking now you want me to get on with it, right?

When you're ready, just turn the page, and I will begin my story ...

Chapter
1

Once upon a time, long ago, there lived a gifted silversmith with his family in Hillsborough, North Carolina. His name was Roswell Huntington. On 15 March 1763, Roswell was born in Norwich, Connecticut to his young parents, Ebenezer and Sarah Edgerton Huntington. When he was almost a year old, Roswell's father died mysteriously in the West Indies. Ebenezer Huntington was only twenty-three at his untimely death. On 15 June 1765, Roswell's mother married Joseph Gale.

It is unknown as to the reason why his mother never cared for him after the age of six. In 1769, the Norwich court appointed Captain Daniel Throop, a relative by marriage, as his legal guardian. The Captain took Roswell to live with him in Lebanon, Connecticut. Before young Roswell left his teen years, he had acquired two more appointed guardians. His new "fathers" were both from Lebanon and also possibly distant relatives, William Huntington in 1774, and Andrew Huntington in 1777. At age twelve,

Roswell and his guardian William enlisted in the Third Connecticut Regiment in early May 1775, and both were discharged by 16 December 1775. It is thought that the boy somehow served briefly during the defense of New London at the time of the Revolutionary War.

In 1784, at age twenty-one, Roswell became an apprentice to a silversmith in Norwich named Joseph Carpenter. He worked hard to complete his apprenticeship and establish his future trade. Soon, Roswell opened a jewelry store in Norwich across the street from the store owned by another relative, General Jedediah Huntington. His storefront sign read: *Roswell Huntington, Goldsmith & Jeweler.* He was only in business there for one year when Roswell decided to relocate to Hillsborough, North Carolina for some unknown reason. It is possible that there was some indication of a dispute between him and the Joseph Gale family which naturally included his mother, Sarah.

By 1785, Roswell Huntington took in a thirteen year old apprentice named Francis Nash to teach him the art and work of a silver and goldsmith. During the following years, while he continued to work with young Nash, Roswell purchased at least two different lots, along with additional farmland which he rented. His farm was located in the old Quaker community on the Eno River near Maddock's Mill. Also, he acquired at least a dozen slaves at this time. It is thought that he may have used them to help out in his first silversmith's shop and the home which he built for himself on Lot 91 in Hillsborough on Tryon Street.

The tiny ring-a-ling of the little brass bell on the door

signaled that a customer had just entered his store. "Top of the morning to you! Please, come in and take a look around. I'm in the back, and I'll be right there in just a few minutes," the busy jeweler yelled out in his deep baritone voice.

There was no one else in the store while the young lady in a fashionable long pink dress walked from the counter to the table to inspect the beautiful crafted items on display. Her long auburn hair fell from her shoulders while her bright blue eyes accentuated her pretty face. She began to touch several pieces while she ran her hand over the assortment of gold, bronze, and silverware which lay on a black velvet cloth on the table.

Several minutes later, the door swung back as Roswell entered the showroom while sweating profusely like a pig roasting on an open fire pit. He wore a soiled leather apron over his blue wrinkled long-sleeved shirt and black gabardine breeches. His long dark brown hair had fallen from the back of the small leather cap he usually wore to keep his thick mane of hair in place while he was working. A few strands were also protruding along the left side of his face where they slightly covered one of his dark brown eyes. He pushed the hair back from his face.

A bit startled at his sudden entrance, the young lady looked up from the table in surprise while nearly dropping the silver spoon she was holding in her hand. She quickly observed the unkempt store owner, looking rather like a common field hand, while she gave him the once-over without trying to appear so obvious. He was tall and extremely good looking with long slender fingers and big feet.

"I'm sorry to have taken so long, ma'am. As you can probably guess, I am busy working in my shop. Please excuse my appearance," he said.

"You don't have to apologize, sir, I completely understand. I have an uncle who is a blacksmith, and you both look quite the same, I assure you," she replied.

"Good morning, Miss…?"

"Miss Mary Palmer, but I am also called May," she said.

"Well then, May, may I call you May?" Roswell chuckled.

She laughed. "Why certainly, sir, and how shall I address you?"

"I am Roswell Huntington, at your service, Miss May Palmer. Is there anything I can show you in particular? That spoon you are holding was just made last week."

"It's very nice. The engraving is just beautiful."

"Thank you, Miss Palmer. It's going to be part of a special wedding gift that I am making for a young bride-to-be."

"I believe she will love it!" She placed the spoon back onto the table. "I have passed by your store several times, but this is my first opportunity to stop and come in."

"I am glad you did. I've only been open for a few months. The first of the week usually finds me working with my silver production on those days. Thursday, Friday, and Saturday is when I devote more time to the store. You know, if I don't sell anything, it's hard to pay my bills. It takes money to make money," he laughed.

"I certainly agree. My father is Martin Palmer, a planter,

so I know whenever his crops do not produce, he has bills to pay, regardless."

"Do you see anything you like on the table? I have a few pieces in the shop that I haven't put here in the showroom."

"I am looking at the little silver thimble over there," she pointed with a dainty wave of her small hand. "How much is it, may I ask?"

"For you, Miss May, I would only charge you a mere two dollars. It's made from coin silver."

"Coin silver?" she asked.

"Yes, ma'am, you see whenever pure silver that is mined is not always available, then silver coins are melted down instead."

"Oh, I see, thank you for the explanation. I know that my mother would absolutely love this thimble. I believe I will get it for her birthday next week."

"A good choice! I'd be more than happy to wrap it up for you if only I had some paper. So sorry, but I'm completely out of wrapping paper."

"That's perfectly all right, since I'm afraid I don't have two dollars in my purse right now," she laughed. "What am I to do? I'm so embarrassed!"

"Oh, no bother about that, Miss. I will gladly give you a credit and you can pay me later, maybe next week, perhaps."

"Thank you, Mr. Huntington."

"Please, call me Roswell. May I have your address to add to my ledger?"

"Certainly, Roswell. It is 174 Churton Street located down the street from the Hillsborough Presbyterian meeting house. Do you attend church, Mr. Huntington? I meant Roswell."

"I know I should, but no, I really don't have the time."

"I thought you might possibly be a Quaker since your store is in this area."

"My humble dwelling is also quite near. I bought and built my house on former Quaker land, you see."

"My family attends the Presbyterian meeting house regularly. Maybe I could invite you there sometime when you're not so very busy."

"Why thank you, May. You might be surprised to see me there one of these Sundays. Here, don't forget your thimble," Roswell said while she was about to leave.

May Palmer took the thimble from the tip of Roswell's little finger that he held outstretched while she collected her purchase and placed it into her purse as she walked toward the door.

"Have a good Monday afternoon," he called out. "Stay safe and well."

"Thank you, sir, you do the same," she said while the door closed behind her as she left. She smiled with a big grin whenever she looked up at the hanging sign: *Roswell Huntington, Goldsmith & Silversmith, est. 1786.*

Roswell Huntington was smitten while he stood there for the time being and sniffed the fading fragrance of Miss May Palmer's sweet rosewater cologne. He began to whistle while he went back to work.

At age twenty-three, Roswell Huntington was now the same age that his father, Ebenezer, had been when he died. Why that man went to the West Indies, he would never know, and what about his estranged mother, Sarah, and his new step-father, Joseph? Maybe he would see them again one day, but at this time, it seemed rather doubtful.

Three weeks later, early that Sunday morning, Roswell was up from a restful night's sleep. He washed, shaved, combed, and pulled back his hair to almost perfection. He dressed himself in a clean pair of black linen trousers, a white long-sleeved shirt, stockings, and his polished black boots before he went downstairs to the dining room for his breakfast.

"Good morning, sir. Will you be having your usual Sunday morning breakfast?" asked Evangeline, his faithful housekeeper and cook. Vangie was always prompt and proper with him.

"Not this morning, Vangie. I think I'll have a cup of coffee with a lightly buttered biscuit."

"We have fruit if you would like an apple, orange, or banana, perhaps," she said.

"A few apple slices would be nice, thank you. I will be going to the Presbyterian meeting house this morning at eleven. Sunday dinner will need to be served a bit later today when I return."

"I will take care of that, sir," Vangie said while she left for the kitchen. Minutes later, she was back with the small breakfast tray which she set before him. "Will there be anything else?"

"No, this looks fine. Thank you, Vangie."

"You're welcome, sir, and I hope you will experience a most wonderful and blessed service," Vangie said while she left the dining room.

Following his light breakfast this morning, Roswell left the table to go outside and take a stroll down the path to a little creek that flowed along the back of his property. He would usually go there whenever he needed to think about any important decision he was considering, but mostly just to take in all the beauty of nature in a peaceful setting. Presently, he was just killing time until he had to finish getting ready to leave for the meeting house. Without a doubt, he was already thinking about Miss May Palmer. What would she be wearing today? Was she also thinking about him right this very minute? What would he say to her when he finally got to speak to her?

It was nearly time to go when Roswell returned to the house and went back upstairs to put on his tie and get his coat. He tied a royal blue silk cravat around his neck and pulled on his long black waistcoat and buttoned it. He stood back from his full-length standing mirror to take a last look before he left to surprise May. The sun was shining brightly, birds were singing outside, and it was a beautiful day.

Roswell pulled his watch from the front pocket of his trousers while he stood in the vestibule of the Presbyterian meeting house to check the time. He looked down to see it was 10:45 a.m. Five minutes later, Miss May Palmer walked through the doorway while joined by an attractive couple and five young girls whom he assumed were her parents and sisters. She looked very pretty to him while he stood there motionless to see the girl he fancied dressed in her pale blue linen long skirt and jacket. Underneath, she wore a white silk blouse with frilly lace at the neck and a blue cameo pin. A string of pearls fell gracefully through the valley of her ample bosom while a pair of short white linen gloves covered her dainty hands. On her head, she wore a yellow wide-brimmed straw hat tied with a bright blue satin ribbon. Her outfit was completed with a pair of white leather slippers laced up to her ankles. Roswell was quite overwhelmed by her beauty as he stood there smiling and speechless. May walked over to him and extended her hand while he clasped it gently in a warm greeting.

"What a pleasant surprise to see you, Mr. Huntington. Welcome to Hillsborough Presbyterian," May said as they released hands.

"Thank you, Miss Palmer, it is my pleasure to be here and to see you once again. I hope you have been well these past few weeks."

"I have indeed, sir. Where are my manners? Roswell, allow me to introduce my parents, Martin and Priscilla Palmer, along with all my sisters."

Roswell nodded his head toward Mrs. Palmer and the girls while he shook hands with Martin Palmer.

"A pleasure to meet you, young man," said Martin. "May tells me you own the new jewelry store in Market House at the intersection of King and Churton Streets."

"Nice to meet you, sir. Yes, I do own that little shop. I've only been opened for a few months now," Roswell replied.

"I just love my new thimble that May got me for my birthday. It is very nice, and also to meet the man who made it," said Priscilla.

"I'm glad you like it, Mrs. Palmer. My specialty is silver spoons, but I also make jewelry and other small trinkets on occasion."

"I will have to visit your store to see all your work one day soon. I'm afraid jewelry is my weakness," added Priscilla while she gave a pleasant smile towards the nice looking young jeweler.

"Please do, Mrs. Palmer. You are welcomed anytime, but the best days are Thursday through Saturday. May has probably told you not to come at the first of the week because of how I will look on those days," Roswell laughed.

"I do believe that the service is about to start," May said. "Shall we all go in and find our places to sit? We will have plenty of time to talk following the service."

Roswell was invited by Mr. Palmer to sit together in the family box located four rows down on the right of the center aisle. As the service began, he felt unsure as to what to expect from being in a Presbyterian meeting house, let alone any other place of worship for that matter. Roswell had never been taken to any church as a child, so attending services every Sunday up until now wasn't a major concern of his. So, he sat there on the pew beside May and watched and listened. Whenever she stood, he stood; whenever she sat, he sat; when she bowed her head in prayer, he did the same, although he didn't know how to really pray. As the time came for the sermon, he sat up while he began to listen intently, and was quickly caught up in the message about Jonah and the Whale. In all his born days, he had never heard the story of how one man who disobeyed God was swallowed up by a fish large enough for a man to be eaten alive and remain in its belly for three days, and afterward, be spit out upon the dry land and that was his punishment for disobedience. So amazing, he thought as he sat there spellbound over the message. He remembered flipping through the pages of a Bible he once found at home that belonged to his guardian, William, during the time he lived with him in Lebanon, Connecticut. He couldn't remember anything at all that he read at that time, especially anything about the story of Jonah. If he had, he would have most certainly remembered that one. Why that had to be the biggest fish tale he had ever heard in his life!

While the offering was being taken, Roswell's thoughts shifted quickly to May. How old was she? Had she ever been with a man? Did she have a current fellow? How could he show that he cared for her without offending her in any way? These questions kept lingering in his mind until the sudden crash of an offering plate sent coins rolling across the bare floor while he snapped out of his daze.

With regard concerning himself, Roswell knew that he had only been with two women in his life, so far. Once, the first time his guardian, Andrew, took him to a brothel in Lebanon when he was nearly fifteen for his initial experience with a woman. A buxom lady on a squeaky bed that night showed him everything he needed to do. The next encounter happened soon after his leaving the care of Andrew, and being entirely on his own. After a few too many drinks at a party, given by his best friend, Teddy Blackstone, he did a one-night stand with a nineteen year old named Darcy Mae Rainwater. This time, it all began with "you show me yours, and I'll show you mine," and the rest became history that night. Now, the new interest in women quickly peaked within Roswell's loins, although he didn't view "courting" to be as important as his work.

After the service ended, as the small congregation began to file out past the Reverend Macklin, who now stood on the front steps to greet his flock, Roswell pulled May aside to speak with her.

"I would like to find me a Bible, May. Where can I get one?"

"Don't worry about that Roswell, I will get you a Bible."

"Thank you, I will appreciate that very much. May I say that you look very nice today? That shade of blue is definitely your color."

"You look very nice yourself, but Roswell Huntington, you're just saying that!"

"No, I really mean it! You are so pretty to me right now. Would you allow me to call on you sometime? You don't already have a suitor, do you?"

"Well, I will have to confess that I was briefly engaged last year to a man my parents tried to choose for me. There was actually no love lost from either of us, as we both quickly discovered. We decided to break the engagement and move on with our separate lives. We parted as friends, he moved to Virginia, and the last I heard, he had married a young lady with a baby girl. So, to answer your question, I am not seeing anyone right now. Yes, you may call on me whenever you wish."

"Perhaps, I can bring you to church next Sunday if you like."

"That would be nice, only if you promise to come to the house and have dinner with us after service," May answered while her blue eyes sparkled with delight.

"That certainly will fit into my plans. I will see you then, May Palmer," he said with a grin.

"Hey, I've got to run now to catch up with my folks before I get left behind and have to walk home by myself," she laughed as she waved goodbye to him.

"I'll be counting the days," Roswell said while he watched May catch up with her parents, climb into their buggy, and drive away to the end of the block on Churton Street.

Monday mornings usually came early for Roswell as he always tried to be up, dressed, and ready for breakfast by 4:00 a.m. Following a hearty breakfast each Monday through Wednesday, this usually satisfied his hunger so that he never had to stop for lunch. Most of the time, he was so busy in the shop that he could hardly take time to stop, even if he wanted. He started firing up the kilns by 5:00 a.m. each morning, and by noon, he was working almost non-stop.

Malcolm, Sam, Calvin, and a young boy called June Bug were the slaves that worked as helpers for him on each of the three days. If Malcolm or Sam arrived early before Roswell, then one of them would get the fire started. They also helped make the plaster molds and have them ready, depending on what pieces they were casting that day. Francis Nash and Calvin usually helped Roswell pour the molten pure metals into the molds while Malcolm and Sam put them to the fire. If for any reason, sickness or otherwise, each boy was capable of doing any particular job that was needed. June Bug would always do the initial rough polishing while Roswell himself would put the final finishing touch on each piece. An inventory of silver ingots were kept in stock in a small wooden box for daily use; however, when the silver became scarce or out of stock, coin silver would be used in its place. Young Francis Nash was always on hand to work wherever he was needed while he continued to watch and learn all he could from Roswell.

Roswell had his personal trademark as proof of each original hand-crafted item usually stamped or engraved on the back or bottom of each piece, depending on what it was. His mark could be found sometimes on larger bronze or gold pieces; however, practically every piece of silver never left the shop without it. The mark·itself on a small silver piece would appear simply as *R.H.* The larger pieces, which included spoons cast five to six inches in length, would bear an indented rectangular box with the raised lettering *R.HUNTINGTON* on the back. Many of Roswell's unique spoon handle designs were sometimes engraved at the request of the customer. The constant demand for his wedding silver would become his most requested item. Various sizes of spoons and ladles were made for individual sale, while sets of four, six, eight, and twelve became the most popular, especially for any bride-to-be or the wealthy. The sale of a twelve piece set would net Roswell an enormous amount of cash from time to time. Roswell's success began to emerge while news of his business became known throughout the town of Hillsborough while many people took a liking to the handsome young jeweler in Market House.

Orders of bronze and gold pieces were packaged in wrapping paper, while most silver items for sale were placed into small velvet bags with drawstrings. The color choices were red, black, royal blue, or emerald green. These bags were handmade by Roswell's seamstress and laundress, Eliza Dodd, who kept them in supply as needed.

Eliza, now in her fifties, had been sewing most of her life, and was gifted and good with a needle and thread. She had learned to sew from her mother whom she lost from the typhoid when Eliza was a young girl, and now she was quite accomplished as a seamstress. The years had now turned her hair grey around the temples, so she usually wore a brightly colored kerchief or bandana over her hair to help conceal the grey. Naturally, she made all of her clothes and aprons, along with a few shirts she had made for Mr. Roswell in the past. Nowadays, he seemed to prefer them store-bought.

Eliza Jane Dodd was always smiling and happy most days, and it would take something really bad to bring her down. Her only problem had always been a struggle with her weight until two years ago when she finally gave in and just went plump. Being the good seamstress she was, it was never a problem concerning any needed re-sizing or alterations. Eliza had never married, but she had a son almost thirty-two if he was still alive in upstate New York. Years ago, she watched in horror when he was sold and taken away as a young boy from their home in Charleston. Thinking about him sometimes would be the only thing that could possibly make her feel really sad.

Roswell left young Francis in charge of the store on Saturday afternoon when he decided to take the rest of the day off work. Business was slow, and he needed to get home and clean up his wagon to drive Miss Palmer to the meeting house tomorrow morning. As soon as possible, he planned to buy a new buggy, a rig that would have seats for four. Presently, all he had was his old mule Hadley and his work wagon which was usually loaded down with supplies and an assortment of junk. He needed to make it as clean as possible since the wagon was his only means of transportation at the moment, and of course, he wanted to make a good impression. The least he could do right away would be to wash off some of the dirt and grime, and try to find a cushion for the seat.

"Vangie, hello in the house!"

It seemed like no sooner when Roswell yelled out, that Vangie was on the porch as she wiped her hands on a long white apron. She wore a long, blue muslin shift and her hair was pulled up under a small lace cap and tied underneath her chin. Vangie was a small-framed, light-skinned Negress of twenty-three.

"Yes sir, Mister Roswell, I's here. What you doin' home so early today?"

"I've decided to clean up my old wagon this afternoon. Would you please draw me a pail of water with some soap suds and find me a brush?"

"Yes sir, somethin's up all right," she said under her breath. "Mister ain't never clean up no wagon before, not ever. Somebody in love, I's do believe!"

Vangie went back into the house while Roswell unhitched Hadley and took him to the barn. Moments later, she returned and placed the pail near the edge of the porch. Roswell spent nearly two hours unloading and wiping down the old wagon. When he finished, it's unpainted bed and seat didn't appear to look much better, but now at least, it was clean. If he took two chair cushions off the front porch to put onto the wagon seat, it would just have to do. That night before his bedtime, Roswell already had his Sunday clothes hanging on the back of his bedroom door. He could hardly get to sleep at first while thinking about tomorrow. It was nearly midnight, and he was still awake.

Sunday morning came for Roswell much like the previous one a week ago. He finished his toilet, light breakfast, walk down by the creek, and still had plenty of time before he had to leave to get over to the Palmer house. At twenty-three, he felt like a kid again whenever he thought of May Palmer. He still didn't know her age, but he guessed she had to be at least twenty.

Roswell arrived at the house at 10:30 a.m., rang the bell and waited on the front portico. The door was opened by a tall, thin black man, dressed very nicely in semi-formal attire, who invited him to wait in the parlor. Only a few minutes later, May descended the staircase in the foyer and came to stand in the doorway of the parlor.

"Good morning, Roswell. You are right on time, I declare. Perfect timing on your part, and as for me, I am ready," she said.

"You look lovely, May. As you can see, I'm wearing the same clothes as last week, but I did change my tie."

"That's perfectly all right with me. Before we go, I have something for you," May said while she walked over to a nearby table and picked up a Bible. She turned and walked toward him. "Here, I got this especially for you. I hope you don't mind that I inscribed the inside page to you."

"No, I don't mind. Thank you so much," said Roswell while he received her gift with a smile. "May, I have never owned a Bible, and this one is quite special since it is a gift from you. I really don't know what to say."

"Don't say anything, just begin to read it each day. It will change your life and allow you to see things like you never have before."

"What about your folks? Will they be attending the service this morning?"

"Yes, they have already gone. My father is on the finance committee, and he has a meeting to attend before service. Mother and my sisters went along with him, and I'm sure that she will find one of the other wives to catch up on the latest gossip," she laughed. "I'm ready to go when you are, Roswell."

"Now, promise me you won't laugh when you see what you're going to be riding," he said.

May opened the front door and looked outside. "Oh, my goodness, I'm so excited! I haven't ridden in a wagon since I was twelve."

"Sorry, it's all I have right now, but I'm going to get a new buggy real soon, I promise."

"It's fine with me, and after all, the ride is just down the street. Actually, a lot of our members and friends still drive their wagons to church."

Before the service began, soon after they were seated on their pew, Roswell happened to turn through the pages of his new Bible where his finger stopped at the front fly leaf. There inscribed in beautiful calligraphy were written these words: *To Roswell from Mary Palmer – 12 June 1786.* Then down below, near the bottom of the page: *Love, May.*

He felt a lump in his throat while he quickly closed the Bible and placed it beside him. After two hymns, a prayer, a welcome, and three announcements, came the offering and another prayer before the Rev. Macklin stood at the pulpit to deliver his sermon. Today's message was going to be about Samson and Delilah from the Old Testament. Roswell was almost squirming in his seat by the time the good reverend finished sharing the story of Samson. He would always remember that it went something like this while Roswell sat spellbound for the next forty-five minutes.

> *Samson, a judge in Israel for twenty years, caught three hundred foxes, tied their tails together, and set a firebrand to them as he released them into the Philistine's corn fields to destroy their crops with fire. Later, with the jawbone of an ass, he slew one thousand Philistines. Afterward, Samson went down to Gaza and fell in love with a woman named Delilah. Eventually, the Philistines put her up to asking him the secret of his great strength. For a price, she turned on her new husband while she began to continually plead with Samson to give her the answer. Struck by his love for her, he finally confessed his secret. Samson was born a Nazarite, and if his hair was ever cut or shaved, he would lose all his strength. So, his enemies made a pact with Delilah, and came one night while he was in a drunken sleep and bound him with heavy cords. His deceiving wife had slept with him and quickly cut off all the locks of his hair. The Philistines rushed in to awaken their drowsy victim in surprise, while he was totally defenseless against them. They led him away, put*

him in the prison house, gouged out both his eyes, and forced him to work blind at the wheel of the grinding stone. After a long time had passed, Samson was taken to the Temple of Dagon, a pagan god, where he would be mocked, ridiculed, and scorned while nearly three thousand men and women were there to offer their sacrifices. Samson was led into the great hall and secured between the two main pillars of the temple. He asked the young lad who led him to place his hands on the pillars where he may rest. The boy did as he asked. Samson put his hands securely on each one, right and left, stretched out his now powerful arms, and pushed with all his might. No one would ever remain alive to see the long hair flowing down his back. He prayed to his God to let him do this while he yelled out, "Let me now die with all the Philistines!"

All Roswell could say after the service was the same thing for at least three more times. "Those Old Testament men were something else, weren't they? That Samson fellow really did bring down the house!"

Following the service, Roswell and May returned to her house while Mr. and Mrs. Palmer had already arrived. May invited Roswell to sit with her in the parlor until Sunday dinner was ready to be served.

"Papa inherited this big old house from his father. My grandfather lived here with us for almost four years after my Granny passed away. We moved in to take care of him until he died two years ago. Father sold our house across town over on Queen Street, and we've been here ever since. Tell me about your house, Roswell."

"I received an excellent deal on a couple of lots and some

additional farm land when I first moved to Hillsborough. I lived at King's Tavern Inn on Wake Street until I started to build my house on Lot 91 located on Tryon Street. It has been, and is presently a work in progress, I must say."

"What do you mean?"

"Well, the house isn't finished, not completely. I started it as a five room structure with a parlor and dining room separated by a small foyer with two bedrooms upstairs. The kitchen is attached to a breezeway that is connected to the back porch."

"Sounds like the perfect place for a single gentleman."

"Yes, it is for me, but I want to build a wash room at the end of the porch and add running water later on. Right now, the privy works good since it's only me."

"I would love to see your place. That is, if you wouldn't mind showing it to me sometime."

"Certainly, I will be happy for you to see it."

"Since I've shared a little about my family, and you've already met my parents, would you tell me about your family?"

"Well, May, what little I can remember is not that much to tell. I never knew the reason why my father, Ebenezer, left home to go to the West Indies. Maybe it was to get away from my mother, who knows? Anyway, he died there when I was less than a year old. He was just twenty-three, the same age I am right now."

"Oh my goodness, I'm sorry to hear that, Roswell."

"My mother, Sarah, married Joseph Gale in 1765, and I lived with them in Norwich until I was six years old. During that time, she had my half-sister, Sarah, who was born in

1768. The next year, I was sent to live with my guardian, Captain Daniel Throop in Lebanon, Connecticut."

"The year 1765 was also when I was born," May said.

"So, you're twenty-one?"

"I am, Roswell, a 1782 alumni of Science Hall Academy at St. Matthew's."

"I never finished school, that is graduated, but I went to a public school through the 8th grade. I started really young as an apprentice to Joseph Carpenter in Connecticut."

"Do you ever see your mother and the rest of the family?"

"Not really, it's been quite some time ago that I got to see any of them. I guess it was in 1784 when I left Connecticut to move here that I saw my mother for the last time. She had a house full of kids and was pregnant again for the sixth time."

"Did you see your stepfather while you were there?"

"No, not since I was a small child. Most likely he was at work back then. She never told me what he did for a living."

"Surely, he must have had a good job to support a wife and six children."

"My sister, Sarah, sent me a letter just a few weeks ago to ask me how I was doing. She listed all my brothers and sisters with their birthdays for me. I kept the letter, but never responded back to her. I wouldn't know those little rag muffins if I saw them."

"Maybe you can reach out to them, get to know them, I mean later on, perhaps."

"I'll have to think about it, and that's all I can promise or say right now. None of us really have anything in common anymore."

The door quietly opened while Clarence the butler stepped into the room. He stood tall before them while the heels of his black polished shoes slightly clicked together.

"Mr. and Mrs. Palmer request your presence in the dining room where your dinner will be served."

"May I escort you to the table, Miss?" Roswell asked while he stood from the settee and offered his arm to her while they began walking toward the dining room.

"You certainly may, Sir," she replied as she stood and placed her hand onto his forearm, but then quickly slid it down while her fingers interlocked with his.

"It is our pleasure to have you join us for dinner, Mr. Huntington," said Martin Palmer.

A Sunday afternoon couldn't get much better. Roswell smiled and squeezed her dainty hand.

Chapter 2

Roswell Huntington pulled the shade and locked the door in Market House after his last customer left the store at mid-afternoon. He picked up the letter on the counter and dismissed Francis Nash for the rest of the afternoon while he went back into the shop to be alone. He sat on a small oak stool and re-opened the letter to read once again.

15 November 1787

My Dearest Brother Roswell,

It is with my deepest sorrow that I share the dreadful news that our mother has so mercifully died. She passed from this life on the morning of 24 October following a rather lengthy illness. Mama was only forty-four years old. She never was the same following the birth of Polly almost two years ago. Now, I have Polly to look after as well as all the others. Papa is hiring us a cook and housekeeper who is supposed to be here next week before Thanksgiving. It will be a welcomed relief to me since I am only nineteen years old this past year.

I regret I didn't contact you immediately, but I know you probably wouldn't have been able to come to the funeral. There was nothing at all that any of us could have done for her during that last week of her life. The doctor told us after she went into the coma that she no longer suffered.

I loved her so much, and she was a good mother to all of us: Joseph, William, Mary, John, Polly, and me. Roswell, I wish you could have known her like I did. In her own way, I felt she loved you, too.

The funeral was nice and she is buried at St. Mary's in Norwich, if you ever want to visit her grave. I'm in hopes that the next time we are in contact, it will be under a more pleasant circumstance, my dearest Roswell.

Your loving Sister,
Sarah Gale

Roswell folded up the letter and put it into his shirt pocket. He retrieved his coat from the peg on the back door while he threw it across his arm, locked the door, and started the short walk home. Upon arrival, he headed straight to the creek on the back of his property and took a seat on his favorite rock. As he gazed across the flowing stream, his eyes moistened and a single tear fell while it ran down his cheek. He thought about his mother, Sarah, and May Palmer while he pondered his future in Hillsborough. It was almost dark when Vangie approached him on the creek bank.

"There you be, sir. I gettin' a little worried 'bout you. Come on in, I's got your supper ready."

He didn't say anything, but slowly stood up and followed her back up the hill and into the house. While he sat at the table and picked at his food, his thoughts flashed back to Sarah Gale as he wondered how she would look after all these years.

Roswell Huntington knew that out of the nearly two hundred residents of Hillsborough, there were a few wealthy families, but most were just the average rugged and industrious citizens who were honest, law-abiding, God-fearing people, just trying to hack out a living. The town itself was platted into lots with the streets named Nash, Occonechee, Hazel, Wake, Churton, and Hillsboro Avenue that ran north to south, while the streets called Commons, Orange, Union, Queen, Tryon, King, and Margaret Lane ran east to west.

There were a number of public buildings which included the high sheriff's office, among various other offices and shops in Market House, the courthouse, a general store and mercantile, Science Hall Academy at St. Matthew's, a cemetery, doctor/dentist office, the Presbyterian Meeting House, plus three taverns and inns, The Blue House, The Tavern (later renamed Faddis Tavern), and the Kings Inn Tavern. Scattered up and down on lots all over town were a number of charming, quaint, and comfortable homes built by the townspeople who weren't quite ready to support schools and churches at this time. Roswell knew his first home was far from any mansion he had ever seen, but it was very comfortable and provided a roof over his head for him, Vangie, Eliza Jane, Francis Nash, and the ten boys living out back in the little three room cabin they all helped Roswell to build. He kept wondering how May was going to like this set up.

Over the next few Sundays at the Presbyterian Meeting House, Roswell experienced his own baptism by sprinkling, followed by the Lord's Supper and Communion with his fellow church members, brothers, and sisters in Christ. By summer's end, he had added four more rooms to the back of his house, his jewelry store business was flourishing, and he felt he was ready to make the next step. He vowed that the proposal he was about to make would last for a lifetime.

Roswell Huntington married Mary (May) Palmer on 12 October 1789. Rev. Thomas Macklin performed the wedding ceremony at the home of the bride's parents, Martin and Priscilla Palmer, with her five younger sisters in attendance, along with Francis Nash. Their wedding night was spent at the Blue House in Hillsborough. At twenty-six and twenty-four, the young couple eagerly began their new life together.

The following months were spent as a labor of love while Roswell re-structured his entire house to accommodate his new bride. Francis Nash was given the attic for his room while Roswell moved his bedroom furniture, he now shared with May, down to the main level into the largest room he had recently added to the house. With May now secretly being in the family way, she no longer would have to exert herself by the trip up and down the staircase. Eliza and Vangie were given separate rooms across the hall at the rear of the house. At this point, Roswell was glad he decided to build on the extra rooms several months earlier.

May took over running the household since her husband was working at his shop and store most of the time. She was used to having slaves in the house and she got along with Vangie and Eliza very well. Vangie still prepared most all the meals; however, May either helped or cooked some of the simple dishes herself. Vangie taught her a lot about cooking while May enjoyed working in the kitchen whenever she felt like it.

"Well, it's finally happened, my love," May said while Roswell took a seat at the supper table.

"What's that, my dear?" he asked.

"The reason I have been so sick these past few weeks. Roswell, I'm pregnant and you're going to be a father."

"Oh May, what wonderful news! I'm so happy for you, for us, I mean," he said with a big grin. Roswell got up from the table, walked around to where she was seated, and leaned down to caress her shoulders and kiss her waiting lips. "When is this blessed event?"

"Probably in May or June, I'm not sure, only guessing."

"Now darling, I want you to be extra careful around the house. Don't do anything to strain or exert yourself, you hear me?"

"Yes sir, Dr. Huntington!" she laughed. "Did you know that women have babies all the time? Besides, I have 'Liza and Vangie around me, practically all the time, so don't worry yourself over me. You just keep on selling your nice jewelry and beautiful silverware while that will make me happy, my love."

In 1790, May gave birth to a daughter named Sarah, followed in 1792 with a son they named William. Family life was good and things were going well with the Huntington's of Hillsborough. Francis Nash had completed his apprenticeship and left the house to go out on his own. Malcolm, Sam, Calvin, and June Bug remained with Roswell for several more years while the other boys had left out on their own or simply ran away.

In 1793, Roswell Huntington had the distinct honor as he was commissioned by the University of North Carolina at Chapel Hill to create and engrave the cornerstone plaque for the building later called Old East. This structure was the first building erected on the campus of the newly established university. Roswell made the plaque of bronze with the measurements of one-eighth of an inch thick, five and a quarter inches wide, and seven and a half inches long. The plaque was inscribed both in English and Latin with his mark at the bottom – R. Huntington, Sculpt. It is unknown how much he was paid for this work.

Evangeline and Eliza Dodd served the Huntington household for a number of years, at least during all of May's child-bearing years – Priscilla born in 1796; Martin Palmer born in 1797; Nancy born in 1800; Elizabeth born in 1801; and John born in 1808. All three of Roswell's sons, William, Martin Palmer, and John eventually worked with their father until they became silversmiths in their own right.

William Huntington, the oldest son, began making plans for his future in Hillsborough at age twenty-three. He was a very eager, ambitious, and adventurous young man, who like Roswell Huntington, was also a gifted silversmith while having learned his trade from his own father. William ended his studies at the Hillsborough Academy while only completing the eighth grade, but long before that, he was already working with his father at his shop in Market House.

William was a young lad of average height and weight with dark brown hair and eyes, much like his father. He had a few friends that he kept in touch with on occasion but no really close boy or girl friends. He didn't have much time to be involved with lots of social events since he was usually working in town at the shop. He had a pleasant disposition, was well-mannered, honest, dependable, and always seemed to keep a smile on his rather handsome face.

It was during this time, William felt he wanted to try to make it happen by starting his own shop. He knew that he wouldn't actually be in competition with his father, so the way he saw it, they would have the possibility of having two locations to compete with the other jewelers in town. William would have to talk to his father about this situation because he was more than ready to make his next move. Now, he just had to catch Roswell in a good mood, probably right after supper this evening when he was really tired and wouldn't feel much like arguing if it should come to that, hopefully not. William patiently waited for his chance right after the meal while he watched his father push his chair back from the table. Roswell excused himself and headed into the parlor where he took a seat in his chair beside the fireplace. William quickly followed him into the room and stood nervously before him.

"Papa, do you have a minute to talk with me, sir?"

"Certainly, my boy, what is it you want to talk about?"

"I've been doing a lot of thinking lately, and I would like to know how you feel about the possibility of opening another store?"

"Another store? Son, it's all I can do to keep up with the one I got!"

"No, Father, this would be my store; I would simply own and operate it myself."

"Just how do you think you're going to be able to get a shop up and running, Will?"

"Well sir, I was hoping that you would let me fire up my pieces in your shop until I am able to have my own kilns and equipment for the new shop set up to begin production. I would try to rent a retail space in a building in town, a store to sell my jewelry and silverware items."

"How do you propose to finance this new business venture, may I ask?"

"Sir, I have a little money saved up from my allowance while I've been working with you. I can use that as a start to rent or lease the space for my new store. I was hoping that you could loan me some of the money I need to get started until the business is on its feet. It may take me a while to do this this, just so you know, but I would promise to pay you back as soon as I can, sir."

"So, you seem to have it all figured out, do you?"

"I think I do sir, but only with your consent, help, and financial approval."

"Let me get this straight, son. You want to create and make all your pieces in my shop to begin and showcase them in a store that you will own?"

"Yes, Sir! We can bring Martin Palmer in to work with

us, if you will let him. He's old enough now to start learning, too, just like you've taught me all these years. The three of us can make it work, don't you think?"

"When are you planning to do all this? You're not leaving home, are you?"

"Right away, sir. If I can locate the right place, I may be able to have a place to live in the back of the store. What do you think?"

"Your mother is not going to like you moving out, I'm afraid."

"Papa, I'm twenty-three years old. Don't you believe I have a right to decide what I want for my life? I will be living in town, for Heaven's sakes! I am not leaving Hillsborough to go out west or anyplace like that."

"I know, son, but try explaining that to Mama!"

"This may sound like a bad idea to you both, but I'll be damned if I won't at least give it a try!"

"Don't take that tone with me, young man! You know I will not tolerate that kind of language!"

"I'm sorry, sir, please just give me a chance."

"You seem pretty sure of yourself, son."

"I am, and you'll see just what I can do. You, yourself, have told me many times over how good I am working with all the different types of metal."

"If you are that confident, how can I say no to my best right hand man? In the morning, we will go see Robert Eaton and see if he can get us a good deal on a place for you in town."

"What about mother? Do I have to tell her my plans right away?"

"Don't worry, I'll have a talk with your mother."

"Oh, thank you sir! You won't regret this, I promise," William said while he shook his father's hand, smiled, and left the room.

Two weeks before Christmas in 1815, William was set up in his very own silversmith shop in Hillsborough. His new store was everything he had pictured it would be, and now he seemed to be living his dream. *Huntington Jewelry* was located next door to his great-nephew's business, *David Yarbrough & Company,* in the upstairs suite above *Cabot's Mercantile* on West King Street. The rent was affordable and the small shop featured space for a long counter and display case which William built from oak, a small desk and chair, and the back room which would serve as his living space while he was there. He was already thinking about somewhere else to set up housekeeping. To the right of the entrance door was a window box with a large pane of glass that some people called a picture window. In the storefront window, William had constructed a three-tiered shelf on which he had glued a fabric of black velvet to display his fine assortment of jewelry during the hours of operation. He had a large valise to store his beautiful collection whenever he closed the store each evening.

While William continued to work with his father, he kept the same days and hours. Roswell, Martin Palmer, and William would be at the shop Monday through Wednesday, while William alone would return to his store from Thursday through Saturday. The other jewelers in town didn't really appreciate the fresh new upstart while he would continue to beat their prices by running special sales and offering credit. After several months in the business, William began to see a considerable profit. He, along with his father and brother, continued to work hard together to meet all the orders in demand from all their customers. Soon, it became very fashionable in many households to own and use silverware made by either R. Huntington or W. Huntington. After the first year, William was able to re-locate his store to Wake Street with the addition of a small shop in back that housed all the tools and equipment he needed for his business as a successful silversmith. Roswell was proud of both his sons, but especially William, who was now looking at either renting or buying a house for himself.

It had already been a year since his sister, Priscilla had married Thomas Wallis, and now Sarah, who had been engaged for the past year, was getting married to George Clancy. Roswell and May were now down to four children living at home: Martin Palmer, Nancy, Elizabeth, and John. William had bought a large house on King Street while he began courting the attractive daughter of John and Patsy Yarbrough Howze. She may have been part of the reason why William began to attend the new Hillsborough Presbyterian Church, while he also became good friends with the new pastor, a young man named John Knox Witherspoon. Unknown at the time, William was set to begin one of the greatest and long lasting spiritual experiences of his life. On 27 May 1819, he made his decision to join the Presbyterian Church and be baptized. He continued to see the Howze girl to the point of becoming engaged while they both had become regular members in attendance each Sunday at church. William strictly observed his only day off on Sunday, the Sabbath, as the Lord's Day.

In the Roswell Huntington home across town, May fainted when she got the news that baby girl, Elizabeth, had run away and married Charles Parish. Sarah, who had been visiting with her mother, somehow managed to let slip what she knew about her sister's wedding in her conversation while the two were in the garden.

"If I remember correctly, Mama, I believe you were just a young girl yourself when you married my father. Liz is already eighteen, I believe," Sarah said while May Huntington couldn't say anything as she quickly revived and tried to change the subject.

On 9 December 1819, a small family gathering took place at Hillsborough Presbyterian that afternoon while the young Rev. Witherspoon officiated at the wedding of Mr. William Huntington to Miss Frances Robeson Howze, a bride of seventeen. Frances was a beautiful bride, dressed in a long-sleeved, high-collared, ivory gown of satin and silk that had been her mother's. The dress featured a bustle on the back of the full length gown which fell to the floor. Her long brown hair was pinned and piled upon her head in curls with ringlets down the sides of her glowing face with rosy cheeks and alluring brown eyes. A fingertip veil of imported lace was fastened to a Juliet cap which covered her face as it fell to her waist. She carried a bouquet of white roses, mixed with white lilies, English ivy, and tied with a large white satin bow. Mr. Howze gave his daughter away that afternoon to William as witnessed by the entire Huntington family and her mother, Patsy. The wedding was followed by a small reception in the church hall. An undisclosed honeymoon was spent enjoyably overnight somewhere in town following the return of Mr. and Mrs. William Huntington to their home at Lot 24 on King Street the next day.

During this same time, William had acquired at least three slaves, two of which lived in the house with him and Frances while the young boy named Jed Harper stayed in the back room of the store. Ariana Weston was their housekeeper, and Matilda Johnson was the new cook. Ariana, now in her early forties, had come over from Charlotte after she was sold on the open market. She was petite and light-skinned with almond shaped dark brown eyes, and possessed a very pleasing personality. Matilda, on the other hand, was quite her opposite. Tilda was almost sixty, very dark-skinned, with rather large bulging eyes, and didn't mind saying what she thought, at times. They each had a room to themselves at the back of the house. Naturally, Frances took over the complete control of her house, and very much like her new husband, she was strictly business most of the time. She was a strong woman who remained loyal, faithful, and loving to most everyone she met. William always described his wife as "what you see is what you get." He loved her very much.

Early in the year of 1820, William formed a partnership with John Van Hook in the jewelry business. This endeavor didn't last a year since Van Hook was not a silversmith. By November, John dissolved the partnership and went his way to join James Child and Thomas Clancy to sell dry goods, hardware, and cutlery. William continued the business by stocking a handsome assortment of watches, jewelry, and silverware, as well as providing the services for engraving and repair work. He offered low prices for items on sale for cash or credit to those who gained his trust and approval.

Also, that year Frances became pregnant with their first child. William was elated at the news when she told him one night after they had retired to their bedroom. Following the birth of the baby later that year, the excited couple named their new son, John Witherspoon Huntington, after the pastor they both so deeply loved. Little John became the center of attention to both of them while William could hardly wait each working day to get home to see his son. On the morning of 31 October 1821, sudden tragedy struck the Huntington household. Ariana discovered the baby, motionless, cold, and not breathing in his crib. John Witherspoon lay dead at eleven months old. A crib death, although at this time was rather common, still could not have been anything more shocking to the young parents. William felt deeply troubled for days while Frances went to bed for a week. William buried little John in an unmarked grave known only to him at the time. "Life goes on" is all he would say while he and Frances struggled to get on with their lives. Hopefully, there would be more children in the future.

By 1822, William continued to enlarge his growing inventory. In addition to silverware, watches, and other jewelry items, he added gravestones. At first, he purchased eight pair of granite stones for graves that measured from two to four feet long and wide enough to provide any desired inscription usually engraved on the gravestone markers.

The carved out stones were mined locally from a quarry located about eighteen miles away from Hillsborough and were already cut to their precise measurements. They were a light grey color and slightly inferior to marble which made them more affordable. William charged four to ten dollars per pair depending on the selected size, plus the cost per letter for the engraving. One would have thought William Huntington to be Jewish since he always seemed to be looking for something to buy and sell. Regardless, *Huntington Silversmith & Jewelry* was keeping Frances and William supported in the lifestyle they had now become accustomed. Things continued to go well in the Huntington family. William's brother, Martin Palmer Huntington married Susan Holden that summer in 1822.

The news that Frances had delivered her second son on 14 July 1823, was well received by an outpouring from family, friends, and neighbors everywhere. She had the baby at home following almost nine hours in labor. Her last hour was spent on the birthing chair that had been placed into the bedroom while Ariana attended the delivery assisted by Tilda. Afterward, as she lay in bed while holding and nursing her baby, Frances looked as if she had never gone through such a long, grueling ordeal. Her hair was combed to perfection, her color had returned, and she was dressed into a clean fresh cotton gown of pale blue. William arrived home about two hours after delivery, and he was so excited to hold his newborn son. They named their baby, William Henry Huntington, while most likely he would be called William H. to distinguish him from his father who did not favor his boy to be called Junior. Long after the birth of William H., the weeks turned into months, and months became several years while it appeared there would be no more children. Frances seemed perfectly content to care for her one and only son while he grew into a strong, happy, and healthy baby.

Shortly after the birth of his son, William became involved in several new partnerships that would include travels to other towns at times. He, along with his brother Martin Palmer, formed a number of short-lived partnerships that kept them traveling to and from the nearby towns of Milton, Oxford, Salisbury, and Charlotte. Before teaming up with the Virginia born silversmith, Thomas Trotter in Charlotte, William and Frances were in for an unexpected surprise. In all his weeks, back and forth to Charlotte, and only home for a brief visit, it happened once again. Frances was pregnant. On 25 April 1827, she gave birth to their third son, Isaac Howze Huntington.

For reasons known only to him, in May 1828, William Huntington sold his silversmith business, including all tools and materials, to twenty year old Lemuel Lynch of Hillsborough. The young Mr. Lynch was energetic, industrious, and eager to take over this new business opportunity for himself and his fiancé. He was presently engaged to marry Miss Margaret Palmer, the granddaughter of Martin and Priscilla Palmer on 25 September 1828.

In August, William re-opened his store now located in his home, while he continued to sell his elegant assortment of watches, jewelry, and silverware. William Huntington used at least four different touch marks on each piece of silver he created and sold. Two of the main ones included a simple *W.H.* in a rectangular cartouche with straight corners, and *W. HUNTINGTON* in like fashion. His mark of W.H. should not be confused with that of silversmith William Homes of Boston (1763) who used his initials in a rectangle without the pellet.

William spent his last three years living in Hillsborough while he joined in working with Lemuel Lynch at his shop. He was instrumental in helping young Lynch to become established as a gifted artisan in the field of gold and silver. As a result, his teaching turned the young man into a very successful craftsman.

The year of 1831 provided three major events in the life of William, who was now thirty-nine. First, his fourth son, Duke Howze Huntington was born on 17 January that year. Now, as a father of three living young sons, William continued to operate his jewelry business from home as well as serving for the past twelve years as the town commissioner of Hillsborough, and ten years as the manager of the Orange County Sunday School Union of North Carolina.

The second event was the wedding of his sister Nancy to William Johnston Hogan. This marriage had reduced the original Huntington family down to three, while now living at home remained Roswell, May, and John.

The last event, although somewhat expected, was perhaps more devastating to Roswell rather than all the children. For quite some time, May's health had continued to decline, and now at age sixty-six, some days she didn't feel well enough to be out of bed. With all the children gone from home now, except for twenty-three year old John, her total care depended on Roswell and her personal maid, a slave named Delce.

No recorded documents or papers were ever found to exist in a Bible, family letters, or courthouse legal documents that could provide the date and cause of death for Mary Palmer Huntington. All that Roswell could ever recall years later was that his beautiful May had passed sometime between the years 1831-1833 in Hillsborough. Roswell Huntington remained a grieving widower during this time when he received the news of the death of his step-brother, John Gale, age 52, in Norwich, Connecticut. There was to be no grief for a man he never knew.

Roswell Huntington, now at sixty-eight, remembered his son William saying "Life goes on" while he sat alone on his front porch and thought about the future with his precious family.

Chapter 3

Perry County is part of Alabama's Black Belt region, and is located in the western central part of the state. Its area covers approximately 719 square miles of diverse territory. The northern forests which trail the end of the Appalachian Mountains shift toward the south through its hills and valleys while heading toward the grass-covered prairies and farmland of the Black Belt. The county is surrounded by Bibb County to the north, Chilton County to the east, Dallas County to the southeast, Marengo County to the southwest, and Hale County to the west. The Cahaba River runs through the middle of the county while its tributaries provide many scenic views as well as its natural resource for water and fishing.

On 13 December 1819, the Alabama legislature founded Perry County from land acquired from the Creek Indians in the 1814 Treaty of Fort Jackson. It was named for Commodore Oliver Hazard Perry of Rhode Island who was considered a hero during the War of 1812. After the county was officially opened to settlement, eager pioneers came from the Carolinas, Georgia, and Tennessee to take advantage of its rich soil for farming and multiple business opportunities while the new towns began to develop in the area. The first towns were: Perry Ridge, Uniontown (originally known as Woodville), Heiberger, and Muckle's Ridge, which later became the town of Marion.

In 1817, Michael McElroy, also known as Michael Muckle, cleared a few acres of land and built himself a cabin in the area. By the next year, more and more pioneers began to settle all around him in his namesake little town. Michael Muckle must have felt crowded out after this, so he sold his little cabin to Anderson and Cecelia West in 1818, and moved to Mississippi. Later, the town's name was changed to honor Francis Marion, the famous "Swamp Fox" of the American Revolution. By 1820, Anderson West and his nephew, Solomon West opened the first store in the town called West Mercantile.

The first courthouse was built at Perry Ridge. It was a simple log cabin located approximately seven miles southeast of Muckle's Ridge (Marion). It was soon determined that a more centrally located courthouse was needed, so it was moved from Perry Ridge to Marion in 1823. The new courthouse was now a two-story log cabin that was used until several years later when a much larger brick building was constructed to replace the original log cabin on site.

As the new decade moved into the 1830's, the town of Marion experienced a major increase in its population. It had been over fifteen years since the Creek Indians had been removed from their original territory and homeland,

and now the land wasn't just a place for its pioneers. People were coming from everywhere – farmers, businessmen, and entire families who were leaving their homes in North Carolina, Tennessee, and Georgia to take advantage of all the new opportunities of growth in Marion, Alabama.

The Huntington family was soon to be counted among the many others who joined in the mass exodus from Hillsborough, North Carolina. Who, then decided to move? Why? Regardless of who actually made the final decision, we know that there were ten members of the Huntington family who moved from Hillsborough to Alabama by December 1833. They are: William and Frances Huntington; their three sons, William Henry, Isaac, and Duke; Roswell Huntington, William's father, a widower since his wife Mary Palmer had already died; Sarah Huntington Clancy, William's oldest sister, now a widow; Elizabeth Huntington Parish, William's sister, also a widow; and Thomas G. and Priscilla Huntington Wallis, William's sister and brother-in-law.

Roswell's daughter Nancy, who married William Johnston Hogan; and his son, Martin Palmer, who married Susan Holden; and his youngest son, John, all remained in Hillsborough at that time. It is unclear if any or all of the slaves went along with them. It was known that William Huntington owned at least nine slaves during his lifetime. This would include the slave known as Delce and her two children whom he bought from his father, Roswell, at the time right before the death of his mother.

William Huntington seemed a little perplexed with worry over a matter that had been bothering him for quite some time, while he entered the back porch of the house on West King Street and pulled off his boots.

"Is that you, Will?" Frances called out from the kitchen where she had pinned down three year old Duke Howze into a chair while she had taken the shears to clip his long curly hair.

"It's just me, Frances," he yelled. "Who else would you be expecting this time of the evening?"

She pushed the toddler back into the chair for the third time. "Don't make me have to call your father in here, little man." Duke straightened up and his squirming came to a halt while William walked into the kitchen.

"What's going on, my boy? Mama got you in a head lock?" He walked over to them to try to sooth Duke's feelings and to kiss Frances on the cheek. Frances looked at him while pointing the scissors directly toward her husband.

"You're next, so don't even think about leaving!"

"I guess I could stand a little trim around the ears when you finish up with Duke."

Frances finished up with Duke and sent him off scampering to go find Isaac while William took a seat into the chair. "You just need a trim today, so this won't take me long to finish up with you."

"That's good," he replied. "I've got something important that I need to talk to you about."

"All right, dear, give me about ten minutes and come back. I'm just about to clean up and sweep the floor. I've already cut William H. and Isaac's hair, so now all my men will have fresh haircuts today."

William left for the bedroom to find his house slippers

and hang up his coat. When he returned to the kitchen, Frances was alone at the table while she sat there sipping a cup of hot tea.

"Well, I've been thinking…," he started while she cut him off as he seated himself at the table.

"Here we go again," she interrupted. "Pray tell me what you're thinking about this time."

"I've been talking to Lemuel Lynch recently, and he's telling me that his uncle had gone down to Alabama and was homesteading a place in Perry County, a town called Marion."

"And, how does all this have an effect on us?" Frances asked with a puzzled look on her face.

"Well, my dear, the main thing that seems so prevalent is the opportunity that comes along with a good price at the right time. I don't believe that Lem would be lying about this to me."

"So, tell me about it, I'm listening. What is this new revelation of yours?"

"First, there is rich farm land available right now in Alabama with large and small tracts of acreage, plus numerous lots in the city to build a business or a house, all at a reasonable price."

"And now, you're thinking about moving?"

"To be perfectly honest, I have been seriously thinking about it."

"What about our life here in Hillsborough, and your business that seems to be doing so well?"

"Frances, people move all the time. Sometimes you have

to step out on faith and go where the best opportunities present themselves. Hear what I'm saying?"

"So, you're asking me to move to that town, what is it?"

"It's Marion, my dear, and I haven't asked you to move, have I?"

"You've certainly hinted at it though. William, what about Mama and my father, and yours for Heaven's sakes? I don't think I could leave them, could you?"

"We could ask them to consider going with us, if it came to that. Hear me, I'm just saying that there is a chance to better ourselves with a fresh start and better myself in my business as a new silversmith there located in the town."

"What about your brothers and sisters? Will they also move?" Frances asked.

"I don't know. I would just have to ask them," William replied.

"Frankly, I believe you need to consider especially now the situation with Sarah and Liz. They are now both widow women, as you well know. Why would they want to leave Hillsborough? Those girls will probably be the ones that end up taking care of your father, don't you think?"

"I will be the one that will take care of Roswell when that time comes. If I could convince him to move with us, he would be a great help in building our house and working with me in the shop."

"Well sir, you'll also have to convince me first, or none of us will be moving."

"I'm just asking you nicely to think about it, Frances. It's nothing that we have to do right away. Allow me to talk to the rest of the family and see what they have to say about it. Would you at least give it some thought, please darling?"

"I know you only too well, William Huntington, especially when you start calling me darling," she laughed.

William didn't laugh, nor show any visible emotion while he stood to leave. "That's it, I'm done for now."

"Wait, one more thing," Frances called out to him. What about all our slaves? What's to become of them?"

"If Papa goes, we only have Vangie since Eliza passed away last year, and he sold me Delce and her two children. Along with them, we still have Ariana, Tilda, and the boys. I would probably have to build on two extra rooms for the three women. At the back of the house, I could put a small cabin there for Delce, Micah, and Cassie, and a larger one for Malcolm, Sam, and Jed Harper. That should take care of their housing. The boys will help us with the construction."

"You've got it all figured out, as usual, I see. Guess I'll go and get started with the packing."

"Don't fret yourself, Frances. I didn't plan to say all this to upset you in any way. Again, I'm just asking you to think about this as a possibility. If the rest of the Huntington clan is against moving, maybe it's not meant to be, a bad idea from their brother. I can accept it if that's the case. I'll talk to everyone soon, and maybe then we can reach the right decision. Now, let me see that big beautiful smile."

She smiled at him while he left the room to go outside to use the privy and do some more serious thinking about his next plan.

William Huntington eagerly made contact with each of his family members to share his feelings about the proposed move to Alabama. It was important for him to speak with his father, Roswell, first hand. William met him at his home on a rainy Sunday afternoon. They sat together in rocking chairs on the back porch.

"Think this rain will ever stop?" Roswell asked.

"Eventually yes, but it seems to have set in for a while longer," William said.

"What brings you here to see me this afternoon on such a rainy day?"

"I was talking to Lemuel Lynch last week and he was telling me about his Uncle Jack. He's living down in Perry County, Alabama, in a town called Marion. Jack has bought himself twenty acres of rich farm land for twelve dollars an acre and he plans to plant cotton. He's also planning to build a big house on his land for his wife and six children."

"So, now you are thinking about going there, are you?"

"Yes sir, I've been thinking about it a lot."

"You mean to go there to work and live?"

"Yes, but I wanted to ask you if you would consider coming with us and moving there. Papa, you would be such a help to me."

"What does Frances have to say about all this moving business?"

"It would be hard for her to leave her folks, but with a little more persuasion, I believe she will abide by my final decision. Frances has always stood by me and accepted my decisions ever since the day we married. I'll admit that I have made some bad choices in my life so far, yet she speaks not a word against them. That's one of the reasons that I love her so much."

"Well then, what do your brothers and sisters have to say about all this?"

"That's exactly what Frances asked me. I haven't talked to any of them yet, and they don't know anything about this. I wanted to talk it over with you first before there's any other mention."

"Before I give you my answer, why don't you find out how they feel about everything, and then come back and let me know. I need some time myself to think about all this, too."

"Yes sir, thank you, Papa! You been doing well?"

"I still miss your mother, son. Hardly a day goes by that I don't think about her. May was the prettiest girl I had ever seen, back in the day when I was twenty-three. I still see her every time I look at your sister, Sarah."

"I know, Father, I miss her, too. She loved us all so very much. I need to go now that the rain appears to be letting up. Frances is expecting me back home shortly. I hope to see you again soon, sir." William left Roswell sitting on the porch while he walked away and headed home.

"That boy is so much like me, it's unreal," Roswell said underneath his breath.

A couple of weeks had passed, while William completed his visits concerning the move down south. He met with all his brothers and sisters, as well as Frances' parents, John and Patsy Howze. The Howze's provided him a positive reaction with their blessing and understanding, although they declined a move for themselves. Hillsborough was their home, and they would never leave it. After a few more days, Frances finally changed her mind, and was now looking forward to the move. Praise the Lord! William was extremely happy over her decision while he returned to see his father. When William arrived at Roswell's that day, he found his brother John sitting with their father in the parlor.

"Hello Papa, and John, I assume you both have already been talking about the move," he said.

"Yes, we have," John answered. "It sounds to me like a great opportunity, but as I was telling Papa earlier, I may decide to come later. I talked with Nancy last week and she told me that they would remain here since her William was just starting a new job. What about Martin Palmer and our other sisters?"

"That's why I'm here today to tell Father about everyone's decision. Martin, since he recently lost Susan after her brief illness, will be staying here, but Sarah and Elizabeth have agreed to move."

"What about Prissy and Thomas?" Roswell asked.

"At first, she said no, but later they both decided they would go since everyone else is going. I just talked with them last week," said William.

"So, I guess that just leaves me," Roswell said.

"Yes sir, it does. Now, with Frances and our three sons, that gives us nine who are willing to re-locate. I'm just waiting on a final word from you, sir."

"Well, son, I'm not going to be left behind. My health is failing and I want to be where most of my family will be, so yes, I will go with all of you. I will sell off what I can and be done with it. Without May, now there is nothing to keep me here any longer. Not even my old mule Hadley, and he's almost ready to have to be put down, I'm afraid. When do you plan for us to move, William?"

"I was thinking about that only yesterday, Papa. Maybe you and I could actually go down to Alabama and check out all our options, and see the place before the end of the summer."

"That's a good idea. We need to see where we're going, that's for sure," Roswell said.

"Everyone should begin to sell what they don't need right away. I'll get the word out to everyone about that. Papa, as soon as we both can sell our houses that should net us enough cash to buy some land or several lots to build on. What do you think?" asked William.

"I was thinking along the same lines, son. I'll check with Robert Eaton and Elkanah Watson in the morning to see if they may be interested in buying both our houses," Roswell said.

"That should get us started for now. It was good to see you, John. I need to go right away. I have a customer coming by the house to pick up a set of spoons. I'll talk to you later, Papa."

The next morning, William sat with Frances at the table while Delce cleared away the breakfast dishes. The boys had not yet awakened, so the two of them had a while to be together alone.

"Would you care for anything else this morning, Mister Huntington, Missus Huntington?" asked Delce, who paused briefly by the table edge.

"You may bring me some more coffee if there's any left," said Frances.

"What about you, Mister William, care for another cup?"

"No thank you, Delce. I'm fine."

Delce was a widow of thirty-one, the mother of Micah who was nine, and Cassie who had just turned six on her last birthday. Delce was a light-skinned, attractive young slave sold off a plantation in New Orleans. She was rather tall with long frizzy black hair which she kept tied at the nape of her neck with a ribbon or cord. She was always dressed neatly, usually in a cotton shift with bright colors and a white apron. Delce had been Frances' personal maid since the time before the death of May Palmer Huntington. In a moment, Delce returned to the table with another cup of coffee for her mistress, and then excused herself where Frances and William could continue their private conversation.

"Papa has agreed to move to Marion with us, along with Sarah, Liz, Prissy, and Thomas," William said while he sat looking into the dark brown eyes of his beloved. "If you count our three boys, there will be ten of us who eventually will be leaving Hillsborough."

"So, practically everyone in the family is planning to leave except my parents, who still choose to remain here," Frances said.

"Yes, my darling, that's their decision for now, but who knows? John and Patsy could change their minds at any time."

"John Howze hardly ever changes his mind," she said.

"He may fool you this time. We'll see, don't worry about it."

"I can't help but worry! They're not your parents, William, they're mine!"

"Well, that's all I know right now. I have given you the full report, my dear. There will be the ten of us, realizing that anyone can change their mind at any time."

"How do you plan to sell our house, my dear husband?"

"Sarah is having an ad placed in the *Recorder* listing her plantation in the newspaper, so I can do the same if Robert Eaton or Elk Watson aren't interested in our house and property. I've already talked to both of them about it, but haven't heard back from either of them."

"Also, what about all my furniture? For instance, the pie safe over by the door was made by my Grandfather Howze. I could never part with it, Will."

"I understand, my dear, but we can't possibly take everything. We'll have to sort out and leave behind the things we feel are non-essential. Of course, we will take your pie safe, china, silverware, and personal items, no questions about that. What I mean are things like this old kitchen table and chairs, we can let them go with the house when it sells."

"This is the part I don't like about the move, having to decide what I can and cannot take. I love everything we have here, and now you say that we can't take it all. We've worked hard for all the things we have, and now my dear husband, you are forcing me to make a decision on what I can keep or leave behind."

"I'm not forcing you to do anything of the sort, Frances. We can talk about this later. Everything will work out, you'll see. Right now, I'm more interested in selling the house."

"How far is it to Perry County, Alabama from here?" Frances asked.

"According to the map I was looking at last week, it is approximately 592 miles to Marion from Hillsborough," William said while he reached for the newspaper.

After reading the advertisement placed by his widowed sister in the paper, William decided to follow suit and do likewise. Mrs. Sarah Huntington Clancy listed her spacious Greek Revival home and plantation of nearly two hundred acres for sale. Three days later, William read his own personal ad in the newspaper.

8 February 1833 – Public Notice

I hereby give notice to anyone who has yet to claim or pick up their individual timepiece for watch repair in my home, please do so while I will be closing my shop at the end of this month.

For Sale by Owner – Lot 24 King Street

Large five bedroom home with 10 ft. ceilings, heart pine floors, and crown molding in ready to move in condition on a three acre lot. Also, included with the property is a three room log cabin, several outbuildings, garden area, and livestock, all at a reasonable price. Please contact for an appointment to see if interested. Wm Huntington

Also, listed in the ad at the bottom were listed three slaves for sale: Malcolm, Sam, Matilda.

With so many businesses and families who continued to leave Hillsborough, real estate was slowly moving at a snail's pace. It seemed like each passing week that another house, business, or property went up for sale. William was in hopes that the housing market would pick up before summer's end. "Everybody's selling, nobody's buying" became the typical phrase on everyone's lips in Hillsborough. William still had not received an answer from Robert or Elkanah, nor had he heard anything about what his father Roswell intended to do about his place. Sarah had only one person so far to come look at her estate. William was left thinking that if no one were to be able to sell their place, most certainly, no one would be moving to Marion. William didn't have much to say at supper that night after Frances and Tilda had prepared one of his favorite meals of chicken and dumplings.

On this same night, Roswell and his son, John, sat in the dining room of their house while Vangie removed the supper dishes from the table.

"I will be in my room if you need anything else this evening," said Vangie while she stood in the doorway.

"The supper meal was very delicious. Thank you, Vangie. Can't think of anything right now, so you may be excused," Roswell said.

"Would you like for me to close the door?"

"Yes, please. Good evening, Vangie, I'll see you at breakfast."

"So, William has you almost convinced to move to Alabama or is that just idle gossip from Sarah?" questioned John from across the table.

"It's not idle gossip, son. We've already talked, and like I told William, I wouldn't want to stay here without him and your sisters since they are planning to move."

"I guess William has already told you that I'm staying here for the time being."

"Yes, John, I knew that, but I hope you will be able to come join us there later on."

"We'll see, Father. Right now, I've got other plans for my life, and that doesn't include moving to Alabama. Please understand, sir."

"Oh, I understand completely. I was young myself once, fell in love, and relished the thought of learning how to become a silversmith. That was part of my dream, along with having the wonderful family I had with your sweet mother, God rest her soul."

"If, and whenever I change my mind, I will join the rest of the family in Marion. Sounds like a good place to settle down with so many business opportunities that William has been telling us. Now, we need to get this house on the market."

Surprisingly, during the next several weeks, the real estate market changed while providing a greater outlook for the prospects of the Huntington family. Thomas and Priscilla Huntington Wallis sold their house to a family moving to Hillsborough from Virginia. Thom and Prissy moved in with her sister, Sarah, following the sale of their house. Elkanah Watson purchased Roswell's house while Roswell and his housekeeper Vangie moved into the home of William and his family. Sarah received an offer on her plantation which she was now having to consider. No offers yet on the property of William Huntington or Elizabeth Huntington Parish, widow of Charles Parish.

By the end of June, Roswell and William were making plans for their initial trip to Marion. They planned an almost five day journey by stagecoach through Charlotte, down through South Carolina, Tennessee, and Alabama, heading south to Selma for the final twenty-seven mile trip to Perry County and Marion.

On 28 June 1833, the stage pulled to its final destination while it stopped in the front of the Marion Hotel on Washington Street. It was early morning while the sleepy town was beginning to wake up for the day. The unpleasant scent from scattered manure on the street, mingled with the smell of freshly baked bread wafting from a nearby bakery, formed a distinctive, pungent odor in the air. Roswell and William stepped down from the coach, paid the two drivers, and picked up their bags while heading up the steps of the hotel and into the lobby.

The Marion Hotel, established in 1822 by Mrs. Anne Smith, was well into its eleventh year of operation. As the wealthy widow of Charles Alexander Smith of Charlotte, North Carolina, Anne invested her large fortune into the hotel business when she decided to move to Marion and build her hotel. It was situated along the town square and located precisely across the street from where the new courthouse now stood. The red brick structure featured a large lobby with an adjoining dining room and public wash room. In back of the dining room was the kitchen, large pantry, and the three room private living quarters for the proprietor, Annie Smith. Upstairs, above the ascending staircase, covered in rich burgundy wool carpeting, were ten modestly furnished rooms with shuttered windows spread across the front of the hotel. Across the hallway, the remaining thirteen rooms at the rear featured much smaller non-shuttered windows, with two of the rooms sharing a wash room between them. An additional wash room was located at each end of the hall. Roswell and William were quite impressed with all the elegant furnishings of the lobby area. It was painted in dove gray with antique white chair rails and crown molding. A large, round-cushioned settee, upholstered in rich burgundy velvet, was positioned underneath an enormous white-globed gaslight chandelier. There were several small tables and chairs placed strategically along the walls with two large, leafy palm trees which flanked the black wrought iron handrails of the staircase. At this particular time of the morning, there wasn't anybody to be seen in the lobby nor behind the long mahogany counter located on the right side of the lobby near the stairs.

"Very nice, indeed," William said to his father as the two men approached the vacant counter and rang the tiny bell which set beside the ledger book. *Ding* went the little bell while its sound signaled the proprietor as she entered momentarily through a side door and came to stand behind the counter.

"Good morning, gentlemen! May I help you?" she asked.

"Yes, ma'am. We'll be needing a room together for a couple of days and nights. This is my father Roswell, and I'm William Huntington from Hillsborough, North Carolina."

"Welcome to our little town. I hope you both will find

everything to your liking. Please sign the guest register, and your rate will be two dollars each per night. You may pay in advance or whenever you choose to check out."

"I don't know exactly when that will be, so I'll just wait until then," said William.

"That's fine, sir. I'm Anne Smith, and I am originally from Charlotte. I came to Marion several years ago and built this hotel with my dear Charlie's money, God love him! I think he would be very proud of me today if he were alive to see the place."

"You have a very nice hotel, Mrs. Smith," said Roswell.

"Thank you, sir. You may both call me Anne or Annie, like most people around here. I usually answer to both. I have a nice room for you next to the wash room upstairs. So, here's your key," Annie said while she reached into a drawer, pulled out key #21, and placed it on the counter.

"When is the check-out time?" asked William.

"Check out is noon each day and we serve three full meals a day. The times are listed on the sign posted on the dining room door. I hope you will enjoy your stay with us while you are in town this week," Annie said with a warm, friendly smile.

"Thank you, Annie. I'm sure we will since I am already impressed with what I've seen so far," William said while he pocketed the room key.

"Anything else that I may help you with this morning?"

"We're here to possibly purchase a tract of land to start a business, and also several lots for the other members of our family to build on for housing. Could you tell me who

I need to contact to show us some recent listings that may be currently for sale?"

"That would be Mr. Niles Chandler or Miss Jenny Lou Phillips. You will find them at Marion Realty, and their office is just across the street. They should be there when they usually open around 10:00 a.m.

"Thank you very much. I believe we will go up to our room now to rest and freshen up a bit. Are you ready, Papa?"

"Yes, son, I'm more than ready. This trip has about done me in, and I believe my traveling days are about over. I need to lay this ol' body down for a spell."

"We will bid you a pleasant good morning, Annie, until we see you again later today," William said while he picked up his bag, and also Roswell's as he motioned his father toward the stairs.

Annie stood there at the counter while she watched the two weary travelers make their way up the staircase. Her dark brown eyes peered over her wire-framed spectacles anchored firmly across the bridge of her narrow nose. She was fair in complexion, but highlighted her facial features with plenty of powder and rouge. For a woman of nearly fifty, Annie was rather attractive, but not considered as beautiful. Her long brown hair was piled up and pinned in a chignon, and she wore a pair of pearl drop earrings. She was dressed in a long, powder blue muslin gown that fell to ankle length.

As William and Roswell took a turn at the top of the stairs and disappeared down the hallway, Annie turned the guest register book around to re-check the names written there. It was signed: Roswell & Wm Huntington,

Silversmiths – Hillsborough, North Carolina. Annie closed the book and turned to go check on things in the dining room. *Marion could use a new jewelry store; I could use a new jewelry store; I would absolutely love a new jewelry store; Roswell Huntington is a very nice looking gentleman.*

It was nearly eleven when William awoke from his nap to find Roswell snoring away on the bed beside him. He tugged slightly on his sleeve until Roswell began to move and open his eyes.

"Papa, sorry to awaken you, but go back to sleep. I just wanted to let you know that I'm going over to the real estate office across the street. Be back shortly."

Roswell acknowledged his son ever so slightly while he made a motion with his head, closed his eyes, and returned to sleep. William pulled on his boots, tucked in his shirt tail, and headed silently out the door and into the hallway. As he reached the bottom of the stairs, the lobby area was deserted with the exception of one elderly gentleman who was seated in a nearby chair. The man was taking a nap while his newspaper lay folded across his lap. His loud snoring evidently broke the silence of the room while William rushed toward the door opening onto Washington Street.

Niles Chandler stood in the open doorway of his office while he poked a pinch of fresh tobacco into his pipe. He glanced up to see a stranger walking toward him from across the street.

"Are you Mr. Chandler?" William asked while he made his approach.

"I am! Good morning to you, Sir."

"Nice to meet you. I am William Huntington from Hillsborough in the great state of North Carolina."

"I know exactly where that is, sir. We have several families who have moved here over the past year or so. How may I assist you today?"

"My father and I are here to see what you have available in lots or acreage. We're both silversmiths and we are interested in establishing a jewelry business as well as housing for our other family members."

"Come on inside and let me show you what we have in our current listings," Niles said while they both entered the office as he took a seat behind his desk. "Have a seat. May I call you William?"

"Certainly, Mr. Chandler."

"Please, call me Niles. If it's acreage you are interested in, we have practically any amount you may want. The best farm land is north of here on the outskirts of town toward Perry Ridge. There are numerous lots in town for local businesses as well as home construction sites. What do you think may be of interest to you?"

"My father is resting over at the hotel. Could you take us later this afternoon to see some property and available lots around town?"

"Certainly, my pleasure, and what time would be suitable for you and your father?"

"What about two o'clock?"

"Come back over and we'll leave at that time."

"Thank you, Niles. We'll see you at two," William said while he stood to leave the office.

The divorced father of two young sons, Niles Chandler

walked William to the door and watched as he crossed the street and walked into the hotel. Niles was a tall, thin young man with long black sideburns and a thin moustache. He had clear blue eyes, thick lips, and pearly white teeth. His skin was a deep tan, bronzed by hours in the sun and his coal black hair was cut to shoulder length. He was dressed in a pair of brown breeches, an ivory dress shirt, and black leather boots up to the knee. His ex-wife, Margo, had taken their twin sons and moved to Selma only last year. It was a rumor that Niles was sleeping with his associate, Miss Jenny Lou Phillips, but that could possibly be just idle gossip among some of the local shop owners.

At 2:00 p.m. William and Roswell Huntington were climbing into the buggy that Niles had waiting for them in front of Marion Realty.

"I thought we'd drive out to Perry Ridge first this afternoon," Niles said. "I think you will be quite impressed with all the rich farm land out there. Will you be wanting to have a lot of livestock?"

"Probably not right away, but we would want a good milk cow," William said.

"I would like a large garden area," Roswell spoke up.

"Well, there's plenty of that you'll be seeing in just a few more miles," Niles answered.

Following an hour long tour of the area, Niles drove his clients back to Marion and turned down West Lafayette Street. He stopped the buggy about halfway down the dirt road. "We are now in the western part of town as you can see," Niles said.

"This area is very close to town, I see," Roswell said.

"Gentlemen, here are several lots situated in walking distance of town that we have to offer," Niles said while they all stepped down to walk the property.

"This is a very nice area," William said. "Don't you think so, Papa?"

"Yes, son, I agree. This may be the best place we are looking to buy since the property is already seemingly surveyed into lots and located so close to town," Roswell answered.

"It is definitely a strong possibility if the price is right. How much for the lot?" William asked as he questioned Niles, who stood beside him while he appeared eager to answer.

"We are asking twelve dollars an acre, so a three acre lot would cost you thirty-six dollars. I could make you a special deal if you decide to purchase several lots."

"That seems fair," Roswell said, "but I need to talk it over with my son."

"By all means," said Niles. "Take as long as you want, but I must also mention to you that this is prime property and this area is selling fast."

"Niles, let me ask if there are any restrictions on multiple family dwellings or establishing a business on the same property?" William asked.

"There are none at present that I am aware. You may build a house for more than one family to live in, although it is preferred no more than two. Also, you may run a business from your new home inside or by the construction of a separate building."

"Thank you, sir. We will certainly be taking that into consideration while my father and I talk it over."

Early the next morning, Roswell and William walked the short distance down West Lafayette to fully examine the layout of the proposed property for sale by Marion Realty. It didn't take very long until the father and son had reached their decision. That afternoon, the Huntington duo purchased four adjoining three acre lots on the south side of the street while they were set to become the newest land owners in Marion, Alabama.

The return trip home to Hillsborough, although proven to be very tiring to both father and son, found them both anxious and eager to share their good news with the rest of the family. The Huntington clan was now set to embark on yet another adventurous move as their lives were about to change once again.

It appeared to look like a moderate, windy day on that cold December morning in 1833 while the Huntington family gathered to form their wagon train to begin their travel to Alabama. The women prayed that it wouldn't rain and for safe travel mercies while Roswell, William, and Thom Wallis finished their last minute inspection of each wagon and buggy load. Weeks beforehand, the families had agreed that any additional furniture and belongings would be left in storage in the barn at the residence of Nancy and William Hogan in Hillsborough. There was absolutely no way to take every single possession on this first move. Frances knew that her treasured pie safe was packed up and loaded, so she was happy about that.

William and Frances had finally sold their house to a

family who was moving across town from Union Street. Since they had not yet taken possession, it was decided to meet and form their caravan at the former home of William and Frances by eight o'clock that morning. William, Frances, and their three young sons took the lead position in a wagon that was loaded to its maximum capacity. Next in line was Roswell, who had hitched his two year old mare to his new buggy that would also carry Vangie, Delce, and her two children. The sisters, Sarah and Elizabeth, would be riding together in Sarah's elegant buggy while Thom and Prissy brought up the rear of the Huntington entourage. William had sold his slaves, Ariana Weston and Jed Harper, to his sister Priscilla and her husband, so they would be riding in the back of the Wallis' wagon.

Roswell's daughter, Nancy, and his son, John, were on hand to share their heartfelt good-byes while Martin Palmer had already met with his father earlier in the week to say his good-bye. After several minutes of laughter, crying, hugging, and kissing, William called everyone together while they formed a large circle and held hands while he asked his father Roswell to lead them in prayer. Following the prayer that the family be granted good health and safety on the trip, everyone loaded up to begin their long journey. Nancy and John remained on the porch while trying to smile and wave until everyone was at the end of the street and almost out of sight. As tears flowed down the front of Nancy's fur cape, she suddenly realized that this could be the last time she would see her father.

Farewell to Hillsborough, North Carolina – 16 December 1833

Chapter 4

It was a cold day in January when William Huntington and his oldest son, William Henry, first set foot on his property that faced north on the dirt road called West Lafayette Street in Marion. Now at age forty-two, William had the responsibility of designing and building the house that would become home to him, Frances, and their three young sons. Also, he would have to make room for his father, Roswell, as well as Vangie, Delce, and her two small children. His mind was filled with excitement and anticipation while William pulled his topcoat tighter at the neck while he urged William H. to keep up the pace while he stepped off a series of roundabout measurements.

While the winter sky began to spit out a few large snowflakes, William stood in the middle of the road while his body felt chilled to the bone from the current weather conditions. Suddenly, he had the house pictured in his mind, and now determined that he would build it with the front facing close to the edge of the road.

With his two widowed sisters presently rooming together at the Eagle Hotel in town, William knew that Sarah and Elizabeth would eventually be wanting a place of their own. His other sister, Prissy and her husband, Thom Wallis, had recently rented a small vacant house across town with the option to purchase and had already moved from the boarding house where they had been living. William's major concern now was to begin to build as soon as possible where his family, Roswell, and the servants could also leave the hotel and move into the home he would build for them. William pondered all these thoughts in his brilliant mind while he and William H. walked hurriedly back to the hotel.

During the next several months, William and his father, Roswell, worked diligently with their newly acquired architect and builder while they discussed plans for the construction of the new house. Jacob Whitehall from Marion had been highly recommended by realtor, Niles Chandler, to help draw up the initial plans. The three men would spend countless hours together in the planning stage while the vision William had in mind began to take place as the first day of construction finally arrived.

The Whitehall Company of Marion was a newly established construction company, owned and operated by brothers, Daniel and Jacob Whitehall. Daniel, the younger of the two, was gifted with interior design while Jacob was the premier building contractor. The Huntington project would be Jacob's fourteenth new house to build in the town of Marion. While they waited on the first load of handmade red clay bricks and lumber to arrive by wagon load from Perry Ridge, Jacob unrolled the plans as William and Roswell looked on.

"I agree with you, Jacob," said William while he took a closer look at each drawing. "The kitchen should definitely be constructed first. I like the way the double-sided fireplace will separate the two rooms, don't you?"

"Yes, a great feature designed by Daniel. That boy has a good eye for detail, even if he is my baby brother," Jacob laughed.

"Show us where you plan to locate the kitchen," Roswell said while he looked across the property.

"Just over there on that flat area of land," Jacob replied while he pointed toward the east.

Within the hour, two wagons pulled onto the property and six hired men unloaded the bricks and lumber on the ground. Another small wagon was dispatched to the nearby creek where several small oak barrels were filled with water by two of the men and hauled back to the construction site. One barrel of water was kept for drinking purposes while the others were to be used in mixing the mortar for the new brick fireplace, chimney, and supports for the foundation.

"I have contracted one of the best brick masons I know to work on this job," Jacob said. "Ossie Lee Brown is a strapping young buck, black as night and strong as an ox. He has worked with me on my last three jobs and he should be arriving here shortly. I believe you will like his work."

It was mid-morning when Ossie Lee arrived on site with his helper, the oldest of his four sons, Ossie Jr. By quitting time that first day, those two had the footings poured and the eight brick support columns in place to begin set up overnight. Tomorrow, they would begin constructing the fireplace and chimney in the center while the six hired men were to saw enough lumber to start the formation of the floor joists in preparation for putting down the thick plank flooring. After this first week, hopefully the framing would begin as the weather permitted.

At the end of the next week, Ossie and Junior had the two-sided fireplace finished while the other workers had the flooring down and the four walls up. A boy named Toby Wycliff and his crew soon began to hoist up the lumber to form the rafters and nail them in place. The only snag in the operation so far was having to wait on the delivery of the tin for the roof, since it was on back order and presently hard to come by. Well known for his craftsmanship, Jefferson Motley was the carpenter who was hired to build the front and back door on site, along with the four large window casings and glass window panes. The original plans called for a small front porch and back stoop, but to hasten the completion for the kitchen, William decided that they could always be added later on. He wanted to get started on the main house as soon as possible.

It was a grueling six months until the first phase of construction was completed on the little cottage with its Greek Revival front portico, highlighted across the front with its uniquely crafted dentil work by Motley. Each working week had its own challenges and setbacks, but in the end, Roswell and William were pleased with the overall outcome and appearance of their new house. William could hardly wait for Frances and the boys to see the almost finished place while he and Roswell walked up the steps and stood on the front porch.

"I was beginning to wonder if this day would ever come," Roswell said while he opened the large unpainted front door and stepped inside the foyer.

William stopped in the doorway. "Yes, Papa, me too," he replied. "I'm pleased that we agreed to add the cut glass panes for the sidelights and transom over the doorway. This seems to be a popular trend nowadays. I'm certain that Frances will love this when she sees it for the first time."

"Son, like I told you, it didn't matter to me, but it looks really nice. It's just something else for Vangie to have to clean," he laughed.

After inspecting the front entrance hall, father and son stepped into the front room on the left, which William designated as the parlor or formal sitting room. The rather large room, like most of the rooms, had eleven foot ceilings and this one measured sixteen by sixteen feet. It had plastered walls that were painted a bright blue color with white pine chair rails. Two large eighteen paned windows faced the front view of West Lafayette Street while two others were installed on the east side of the house. The spacious windows allowed the morning sun to flow into the room while they shadowed the fireplace with its beautiful hand-crafted mantelpiece which was painted white.

"This turned out to be a nice room, don't you agree?"

"Yes, Son," Roswell answered. "I believe that I will enjoy sitting in here by myself or with the family on many occasions."

"So, you want the room across the front entrance hall to

become your bedroom, is that my understanding?" William asked.

"Yes, I would like that if you don't mind," Roswell answered.

"Then, it shall be as you say, the front room is yours," William said while he witnessed a look of contentment on his father's face.

Roswell Huntington's bedroom was almost a mirror image to the parlor, while having the same measurements and features, which included another nice fireplace mantel and white chair rails. The room was painted a rich burgundy color, which was becoming popular in many of the newer houses in town. As it was throughout the entire house, natural heart pine floors had been installed with the possibility of adding several room-size rugs and carpets later on with Frances' approval.

Phase two of the original construction plans created the heart of the house which connected on to the parlor and Roswell's bedroom at the rear. Leaving the bedroom, Roswell and William moved through the exit door which led them into the rest of the living space. Their visual inspection continued while they moved from room to room. While standing in the first room they had entered, father and son agreed that this large area would become the informal sitting room and dining room. Located on the far left, beyond the dining room, was a small room painted in pale ivory that would become the bedroom for Roswell's faithful slave, Evangeline.

Just off the sitting room on the far right side on the west end of the house was a large room that measured sixteen by eighteen feet. This would become the bedroom of William and Frances Huntington. This room featured a painted mantelpiece to look like red mahogany, and plastered walls of pale green with white pine chair rails on each wall. Four large eighteen paned windows lit up the room with the afternoon sunshine. An exterior door on the back wall of the bedroom led outside to the back porch where there was another small room attached on the west side located at the rear of the Huntington's bedroom. William planned to use this additional room with its outside entrance as his silversmith and jewelry business in his new home. His next pressing project was to build a stone kiln on the outside located near the house where he would forge his silver.

The large green colored room on the very back of the house had two large windows that flanked the brick fireplace with its black painted mantelpiece. This would be the bedroom for the boys. There were exterior doors, right and left, leading to both back porches for easy access to outdoors. A flight of steps on the back porch led downstairs to a two room cellar with a fireplace. These rooms were constructed with brick walls throughout with a dirt floor in the main room underneath the house. The larger of the two rooms had two small windows, and the family would probably use this room as a dining room during the expected hot and humid days of the Alabama summertime. Several leftover planks had been used to construct the nice heart pine floor. This room was located directly underneath the Huntington's bedroom and hopefully would remain at a much cooler temperature most of the time. The cellar should be ideal for storing any fruits, vegetables, or canned goods as part of William's initial plan.

The last room is a tiny room off the back porch that will be used as a toilet. It contained a toilet chair, chamber pot, and a small oak dresser. On the dresser was placed a porcelain water pitcher and basin with a stack of folded towels. Just underneath the only window, there was a good-sized galvanized metal soaking tub for bathing.

About thirty yards from the back porch of the house there had already been a privy dug out and built from pieces of leftover pine that had been stacked in a scrap pile nearby. The privy was to be used as a convenience during the day while the inside toilet would be available for night time use for only the family. The servants were expected to use their own personal chamber pots at all times.

Just beyond the back of the house to the left was the kitchen where Delce and her two children would reside in the back room. A stone walkway led from the kitchen to the back porch where the prepared meals could be brought directly into the dining room.

Roswell and William concluded the inspection tour of the house while they padded outside to the kitchen for a last look before leaving for the hotel. It was almost a four city block walk back to the Marion Hotel which had been home to the Huntington's for nearly seven months. When Roswell and William entered the lobby, they saw the place was void of any hotel guests while dismissing the activities of several patrons usually seen milling around in the lobby area. Annie, the proprietor, was at her station behind the front counter while one of the maids was busy across the room as she dusted off a small table. Both men gave a slight nod to Annie as they walked past her toward the staircase.

"Good afternoon, gentlemen! Guess you've both been back at that house again. How are things there?" Annie spoke up while the duo halted at the bottom of the stairs. They both turned their attention back to the nice lady now peering over her spectacles at them.

"Why, yes ma'am! How did you ever guess?" William asked while he gave a slight chuckle. "Things are going well at the house, but there is so much more to do before we will be leaving here."

"Don't worry about giving me any special notice," she said. "Please feel free to vacate anytime you need, but know that you all will be missed. I just wish that all my guests were as nice as your family has been all the time you have been staying here. I really mean that!"

"Thank you, Annie," Roswell said. "You have been a gracious hostess yourself, but rest assured, we will be here a bit longer."

"Have a good afternoon," William said while he ushered his father up the stairs.

"I'm going to my room and take a nap if you will excuse me, Son. My feet are swollen, so I think I will lay down for a while to try to get some relief. Wake me when you and Frances plan to go eat supper."

"We will, sir, and I hope you have a nice nap. Here's your room."

William moved on down the hallway and entered his room to find his wife sitting there and busy with her sewing. "Where are the boys?"

"William H. has them outside and they are playing on the back lawn," Frances replied while she looked up from the chair where she was seated by the window. "Well, husband, you'll have to tell me all about the house."

"Just give me a minute to draw a dipper of water. I'm thirsty. You know it's rather a long walk for a man out of shape to have to walk from the house into town," William said while he put the dipper to his lips and took a few sips. "Papa and I just finished walking through the entire house and property. Everything so far has met our approval, although there is plenty more things to do before we can move."

"More to do?" She sighed. "I thought you told me that the house was finished!"

"Almost finished," he said. "In a couple of weeks we should be able to start moving some of the furniture we have in storage. A lot of the finishing touches can be accomplished once we are completely moved in, you see?"

"I can hardly wait much longer, dear. I am growing tired of living here in a hotel room, and having to go down the hall to use the facilities and downstairs for every meal."

"I know, my dearest, these past months haven't been the best living arrangements, but you see, we are almost ready to finally leave here and take possession of our brand new home. You'll be glad we had to sacrifice a little to gain a nice house of our own."

"Will, it seems to me that you have been building on this house forever. What is there left to do?"

"I have a man coming next week to locate the spot and dig a well for us. Also, the Whitehall brothers will be showing me the plans for a barn and smoke house to be built."

"Where are we getting the money for all these additions?"

"Papa is paying for this out of his account, so don't worry about it. We're not completely bankrupt yet," he laughed.

"Good grief! My Daddy told me there would be days like this," Frances said while she rose and crossed the room to lay down on the bed.

"You worry too much, my darling wife," he quickly fired back. "What's the matter, you don't feel well?"

"I just feel a little faint and need to lay down for a while to rest. I want you to go find the boys and make sure they all get washed up before we go down for supper."

"I can do that and give you a little while to rest. Are you going to be all right?" William asked while he moved toward the door to make his exit.

"Yes, Will Huntington, I'm fine!"

The door closed as Frances listened while her husband's heavy footsteps faded away down the hallway. She lay stretched across the bed while she thought to herself. Wouldn't he really be surprised when she told him that she was pregnant again?

Six weeks later and the construction on the house and property came to a halt. It was time to move and Frances was overjoyed at the news when William finally told her. The majority of all their furniture and personal belongings, which they had brought along from North Carolina, had already been removed from storage and set up in their new house. It seemed as though the only thing lacking was having to pack their clothing into the two trunks and have them moved. With only this small task left to be accomplished, moving day arrived early on a Saturday morning. By late afternoon, at the end of the day, William, Frances, William Henry, Isaac, Duke, Roswell, Vangie, Delce, and her two children, Micah and Cassie, had just about settled into their new residence on West Lafayette Street.

Later that afternoon, William hitched up the wagon while he took Delce with him to go uptown to West Mercantile, owned by Anderson and Solomon West, to purchase enough food items to get them stocked in for a few days. Shopping for groceries was easy this first time because everything was most definitely needed: coffee, tea, sugar, flour, salt, pepper, fresh milk, eggs, and vegetables while Frances' list continued. William was careful to double check and make sure he got everything on her list.

By the time William and Delce had returned from the store, the Huntington household was in full swing while Frances sat at the dining room table while she provided direction for unpacking and getting each room organized. Since she had already shared the news several weeks earlier, being in the family way once again, William forbade her to do any heavy lifting, unpacking, or anything that might cause her to lose this baby or endanger herself in any way. It was all too risky. He was so happy at the thought of having another child, a daughter this time, perhaps.

While another season was about to change once more, the chill in the air ushered in the blustery days of autumn at the Huntington household. With a new barn, smoke house, and fenced in chicken yard and hen house, the three acre lot was transformed into a working farm. With no city restrictions during this time, the property owner could build or construct anything on his land as he saw fit. Also, he could operate a business directly out of his home with no worry, except for the annual property tax at year's end. This information allowed Roswell and William the opportunity to start up their new business venture in Marion as the gifted silversmiths they were known from their former home in Hillsborough, North Carolina.

While Roswell became the overseer and basically ran the estate each day, he also handled the financial obligations of purchases, loans, and the payment of all bills. His latest due bill was for the payment of all the livestock that had been purchased during the past few weeks which included: two mules, a milk cow, two goats, a turkey, a rooster, three hens, a tom cat, and a hound dog he named Jack.

In his spare time, Roswell planned to work with his son as soon as William could get his jewelry shop opened in the little room off the porch on the west end of the house. Frances ran the household while Vangie was the house servant, and Delce was the primary cook, although Frances enjoyed creating new dishes and recipes whenever she felt like it. William Henry helped out with the milking sometimes as well as doing small chores that his mother assigned him. Isaac and Duke were left to help William H. feed all the animals whenever he would make them do it; otherwise, they enjoyed playing with Jack and shooting the sling shots that their grandfather made for them.

It was a hard life, but a good life while the Huntington family became known in the town for their strong moral values, honesty, Christian beliefs, and work in the

Presbyterian Church. William and Roswell Huntington made it their policy to treat every customer fairly and honestly while applying the Golden Rule in everything they did. "Do unto others as you would have them do unto you."

"Son, I was thinking that we could use two or three young piglets on the place."

"A great idea, Papa! We can start building a hog pen in the morning," William said.

Chapter

5

Thanksgiving Day fell on 27 November that year, along with Roswell's sharp ax which ended the brief life of Tom, the turkey. Delce spent all morning while she dressed, cleaned, and cooked the bird that was soon to be the white folk's evening meal. Plans had been made earlier that week for William's sisters to join them for Thanksgiving dinner at the new house. Roswell was pleased that three of his daughters would be joining the rest of the family while he loved to see his girls: Sarah Huntington Clancy, Elizabeth Huntington Parish, and Priscilla Huntington Wallis, and her husband, Thomas. The talk around the dining table that evening centered around the discussion of a family gathering in Hillsborough at Christmas where they had all been invited to the home of Nancy Huntington Hogan and her husband, William. It was uncertain at this time whether Roswell's sons, Martin Palmer and John, could possibly join them there during the holidays. After the bountiful dinner, the men retired to the parlor while the women cleared the table, washed, and put away the dishes.

"I must say that you both have built a remarkable place here in Marion," said Roswell's son-in-law while he took his seat on the blue velvet sofa.

"Yes, Thom, but William deserves most of the credit," Roswell replied. "After all, it was his plan and vision since I am limited in what I can do physically, you see."

"Papa has been a big help around here, and I'm anxious for him to start working with me when I get the shop up and running once again," William said. "How are you and Prissy getting along in the house you rented across town?"

"We're doing well, and thanks for asking. We hope to build or purchase a house of our own in the near future," Thomas answered.

"You know already that we have three more lots down this street, so maybe Prissy wouldn't mind building on one of those three acre lots. We could let you have one if you were to try and convince her," Roswell said while he tried to sense a reaction from Thom Wallis.

"I could talk to her about it, but we really like our rental house. The truth is that we've already decided to make an offer to our landlord to buy it ourselves. We both love that the house is so close to town," Thomas replied.

"Too close to be stuck next to the relatives, I suppose," William chimed in the conversation.

"Oh no, it's not that, I assure you," Thomas said quickly. "We just like living in our little neighborhood on West Monroe Street."

"Papa, what are we going to do with those extra lots?" William asked as he turned toward his father's direction.

"William, I believe that I heard your wife say that she was planning to talk to that Chandler fellow, and ask his help in getting her started in the real estate business."

"Well, that's the first I've heard about that; however, I do believe Frances would make a very successful real estate agent. Whenever she speaks her mind, I've learned not to stand in her way," William laughed.

"Yes, that's true, son. Frances is so much like your mother. I could never say no to my sweet May whenever she would use her soft voice and bat those long eyelashes at me. How I still miss that dear woman so much!" Roswell said while he lowered his head.

"Yes, Mama was indeed a true and gracious southern lady whom I remember always managed somehow to get in the last word."

"I agree, William, but I don't reckon you ever knew how much she valued your opinion on so many things since you were the oldest son. I remember when she had a major discussion with Sarah about her marriage to George Clancy, and May told her 'I need to talk to William about that.'"

"That was probably the last time Sarah attempted to confide anything that personal with your mother," Roswell chuckled.

Prissy appeared suddenly in the doorway while she drew her attention across the parlor toward her husband. "Thom, darling, if you're about ready to leave, I'm not feeling well and we probably need to say our goodbyes."

"Don't go now, sweet daughter," Roswell begged. "You will miss our family stroll uptown later this evening."

"I'm sorry, Daddy, but I really need to get home right away."

Following Thom and Prissy's hasty departure, William and Frances gathered their three small sons while they took a walk into town to accompany Sarah and Elizabeth back to their rooms at the hotel. Roswell decided he would remain at the house since he wasn't feeling well. After a brief stroll along the storefronts, William and his family headed back to the house. Frances, now at almost six months in her pregnancy, was also feeling a bit fatigued after a long and busy Thanksgiving celebration with the family.

The next morning, William had a financial meeting at the church. The Marion Presbyterian meeting house located near Washington Street was first organized on 30 July 1832, and built as a small wooden structure in town. It was the place of worship where the Huntington family began to attend services shortly after their arrival in Perry County, Alabama.

While a young man in Hillsborough, North Carolina, William followed the family tradition of civil service and responsibility. His personal interest in Sunday schools for the under-privileged was typical of his workings in the church. William's first position while elected as treasurer at Hillsborough Presbyterian ultimately led to his ordination as an elder soon after his marriage to Frances in 1819. He was elected as a county commissioner in 1823, and served in that capacity for ten years until his final departure to re-locate in Marion. The local townspeople there soon began to regard William Huntington in high esteem while the young father of three sons proved himself as an honest, hard-working, loyal citizen. Following his meeting at the church that day, William had been elected as treasurer by a unanimous vote of the church council. His dedication as a faithful Christian would follow William for the rest of his days while the man himself maintained a true servant's heart. Life in Marion continued to expand with its new surge of businesses, schools, and various churches, while the Huntington name became well-known in the town and surrounding areas.

The original plan to return to Hillsborough for Christmas that year had to be canceled due to illness in the Huntington household. Roswell seemed to develop a foot ailment that began to plague him with almost constant pain and swelling. Sarah had experienced a couple of fainting spells, while Prissy couldn't shake off her morning sickness. Frances, now at nearly seven months, was too far along to consider making such a long trip to Hillsborough.

Christmas in Marion was spent much like this past Thanksgiving. The family gathered for dinner on Christmas Eve, followed by a small gift exchange among the Huntington boys and Delce's children. Frances always saw to it that Micah and Cassie were never neglected at Christmas or their birthdays, but they were never treated as equals. William Henry, Isaac, and Duke would ultimately remain as her number one priority whenever it came to the children in and around the house.

Although it was never William's intention to ever move back to Hillsborough, he did return there at least twice after his move to Alabama. His first visit was made on 17 May 1834 to settle some of his existing business accounts. Correspondence from the tax assessor in Hillsborough deemed it necessary for William to appear in person to settle the matters over a tax issue. Being the honest Christian man he was known to be, he heartily complied with this in order to reach a final settlement.

The second trip was made just two months following the joyous occasion of the birth of his fifth son who was born on 15 March 1835. Following a stressful delivery by Frances early that morning, Thomas Roswell Huntington came into the world, while appearing as a small frail newborn baby. Despite his mother's hard labor, their little boy was received as another precious gift of God, while William and Frances celebrated the birth of their new son. Seeing that his wife and baby were doing quite well, made it easier for him while William was summoned once more back to Hillsborough during the month of May 1835.

William Huntington and his son-in-law, George Clancy, were named as executors and trustees in the will of the late Martin Palmer, Roswell's father-in-law. Since his daughter, May Palmer Huntington, was now also deceased, the probated will of her father made provisions of his large estate with careful instructions as to its final disposition. Among those provisions, the first mention and bequest of a Negro woman and her children to be provided to May and Roswell were listed and granted to Roswell. At the time of the reading of the will, Roswell had already sold and given the slave, Delce and her two children to his son William on 17 November 1829. Thus, the explanation of how Delce came to belong now to the William Huntington household. Martin Palmer's death at age ninety marked the end of an era in the family while he was remembered for his long life, industrious working skills, and honest character.

Shortly after William returned to Marion, he immediately began to purchase more real estate while Frances dabbled in the business at times, and aided her husband in many of his choices. At this time, he had gained more knowledge about Perry County and the excitement of now living in the new frontier town. William was quick to share with all his family and friends how pleased he was with this country, while he was getting as much work as he could do, and all at much better prices than he ever could imagine. Also, if he could experience a good season of planting and harvesting his newly acquired two hundred acres of corn and cotton in Perry Ridge, this venture would go hand in hand together with his jewelry business to increase his wealth in the future.

Roswell's health continued to decline during this time while he was plagued with the sometimes painful condition of his legs and feet. His legs would throb and his feet would swell until the pressure would almost render him unable to stand or walk for any period of time. He was confined to sit in a chair or lounge on his sofa or bed as an almost certainty, a bad spell could happen at any time. The problem seemed to stem from poor circulation or blood clots. During the past year, Roswell had been a great help to William, while he assisted him when he was working on silver pieces in the shop, or helping to sell their jewelry in the store located on the side of the house. For the last few weeks, the only thing on Roswell's mind was the thought of John and Nancy, his son and daughter, possibly moving to Marion to join the rest of the family.

In the midst of a seemingly prosperous time in the Huntington family, Roswell Huntington suddenly died on 8 September 1836 at age seventy-four at the house on West Lafayette. The coroner's report listed his death from rheumatism in the chest, signifying most likely a heart attack. William was stunned at his father's passing and the death grieved him just as it had when he lost his first born son. The sudden loss of Roswell Huntington was felt as a tremendous shockwave poured out over his sons and daughters, grandchildren, the remaining Gale siblings, and a host of friends from Hillsborough and Marion alike. The sensation of re-living the day when her father made his departure to leave home to go to Alabama, daughter Nancy was haunted by his death for a long time.

A simple funeral service was held at Marion Presbyterian for Roswell as the family and a few close friends gathered to reflect upon his life. The eulogy was delivered by William's former friend and pastor, Rev. John Knox Witherspoon, who had traveled all the way from Hillsborough, North Carolina, to conduct the service. In the casket, the Bible that May Palmer had given her husband before they were married, was placed opened to the page where her inscription was written and his right hand placed onto the page. It was a request that he had made to William, not long after he moved with him to Marion.

William had purchased a large family plot in the Marion Cemetery where he would lay his beloved father to rest, while planning to order the huge gravestone marker of granite that he would himself assist with its engraving. With Roswell's death and burial came the reassurance of what would become the Huntington's final resting place located on the right upon entrance into the cemetery through the main gate. A grieving William Huntington remembered all the good times that he had shared with his father while he sat rocking his son, Thomas Roswell, to sleep that night in Roswell's worn rocking chair.

Life goes on ...

During the next few weeks, some unfortunate business transactions of the family suggest that perhaps Roswell was the most prominent and dependable financial advisor of the family. It was now proving that William, seemingly honest, caring, dependable, and having the forethought for great visions and plans, was not always the best financial genius. Soon, it was discovered that William, and also his brother, Martin Palmer, had over-extended themselves financially on various business deals. Overdue bank notes and unpaid bills kept popping up for both of them while they struggled to make ends meet. It would be quite a blow to William, especially if he were to lose the house and all his farm land.

At the time when William thought things couldn't get any worse, suddenly tragedy struck his family once again. All was quiet in the house early that morning while William and Frances were still sleeping in their bedroom. Duke and Isaac lay fast asleep in their room while William Henry, who had now taken his grandfather's room as his own, showed no signs of waking up anytime soon. The baby lay in his crib in the corner located close to the fireplace of his parent's spacious bedroom. The boy was now two years old and Frances had already mentioned to William that it was time to move little Thomas Roswell into the back room with Duke and Isaac. At the far end of the house, Vangie was awake while the morning sun was peeking through her window. Her mind told her that it was time to get up and moving, but her body said 'no'. So, she continued to lay in her bed and think about all the things she needed to do today, 1 April 1837.

William awoke first, grabbed his clothes from his bureau and the hook on the bedroom door, while he made his way to the wash room to use the toilet and dress himself for the bright new day. After he left the bedroom, Frances got up and as her usual routine, she put on her slippers and robe. She would always walk over to the crib and check on Thomas before attempting to leave the room. Some mornings, he would be laying there awake, moving, cooing, laughing, or sometimes crying if he was soaking wet or hungry. This morning, Frances looked down on a still, motionless, helpless little infant that felt so very cold to her touch and had already turned blue in color. Her bloodcurdling screaming awoke the entire house while William was first to dash back into the bedroom. Following close behind him was Vangie while they both saw Frances as she lay in a heap, now passed out on the floor by the crib. William scooped her up from the floor and placed her on their bed.

"What has happened to our boy?" William yelled out in agony while he looked down into the crib to see his dead son.

"Crib death," Vangie whispered while she watched him fall beside Frances on the bed.

"What's happening in here?" William H. yelled out while he and the boys made it as far as the doorway where Vangie had blocked their way into the room.

"Boys, go back into your rooms and your father will come shortly to see you there," Vangie insisted while they left and wondered why their parents were both laying on the bed and holding on to each other.

Crib deaths were not all that uncommon during this time since this type tragedy had already happened to other families in Marion, and also to two other families that the Huntington's had known in Hillsborough before they left North Carolina. There had always seemed to be this lingering question while it circulated among doctors, nurses, pediatricians, and the general public, hospital statistics concerning the sudden deaths of newborns and young infants. The question, how should a baby be placed when put down for sleep – on his back or stomach? This issue would be determined by each parent of a newborn, while Frances usually placed Thomas on his back to sleep. God only knows why Thomas Roswell was taken that morning while the Huntington family went into deep mourning for several days. William had his son buried just a way down from Roswell, his namesake, in the Marion Cemetery. Later, he had a special marker placed there in the family plot. For weeks, the grief-stricken father would never mention or talk about the death of his son until the day in town when he met Annie Smith on a street corner. She asked him about the family. All he would say was … *Life goes on* …

Chapter 6

Six weeks after the loss of little Thomas Roswell, a series of unfortunate business transactions began to emerge which pitched several family members onto the road of financial decline. It all started with William, who owed a man named John P. Graham, the past due sum of seven hundred fifteen dollars. That very same day, his youngest brother John, signed a note due William Rainey for twenty-five dollars. This is the first indication that John Huntington had now re-located from Hillsborough to Marion.

On a beautiful day in the Fall of the year, William was at home to witness the birth of his sixth son, born on 27 October 1837. Frances had a good delivery with no complications, while she was attended during her labor by Delce and Vangie. They chose to name their baby son, Martin Palmer Huntington, after William's brother. Mother and son seemed to be doing well.

On the other hand, it is unknown where John took up residence upon his arrival, but he is credited with building three houses during the years 1838-1840. The first one, most likely for his bride to be, Salina Gray, whom he married 29 March 1839 in Marion. The house would later be called Belle Terrace because of its sloping front lawn. The next year, John continued with another house located to the right of Belle Terrace on another lot he bought from his brother, William.

Like his father, Roswell, and brothers, William and Martin Palmer, John was also a silversmith by trade. By the time 1840 arrived, he went totally in debt, hook, line, and sinker, while he acquired the lot next door to his brother William to begin construction on the home that would one day be called Myrtle Hill.

The house was a two-story Greek Revival, featuring four Doric columns which supported a double veranda on the front portico which was accented by sets of tall shutters which flanked the front windows on each side. Along with its spacious parlor, dining room, and five bedrooms, the beautiful heart pine flooring ran throughout both upstairs and downstairs. The kitchen was most likely built before the main house construction was started. It was located out back, several yards away from where the house was to be built, along with a carriage house positioned to the left of the kitchen.

At this time, all of the dreams and schemes of John Huntington suddenly came to an abrupt ending while almost leaving him completely bankrupt. Shortly after the construction of Myrtle Hill was complete, he was forced to sell the entire estate for three thousand dollars in order to pay off his outstanding debts that continued to mount rapidly upon him. At the same time, his brothers, William and Martin Palmer, were suffering from their financial obligations from over-drafts, loan payments, and household bills to the point of sheer desperation. Also, their widowed sister, Elizabeth Huntington Parish, had borrowed a large sum of money and was finding difficulty in having to pay back her loan.

On 14 April 1840, the three brothers borrowed exactly $4,273.84 in cash from a man they were acquainted with from Philadelphia who was named Lawrence Heldebrun. The Huntington's put up Lot 15 on Washington Street, four acres on Lafayette Street, and ten slaves as security for the loan. By summer, William Huntington reached out to his friend, Dr. James Webb, who was an agent at the Bank of Cape Fear in a personal letter, while attempting to describe the family's financial problems. Dr. Webb probably never knew about the loan from Lawrence Heldebrun since William made no mention of this transaction in his letter. His main reference centers on the various aspects of their business ventures and the relationship with his brothers.

The following is a copy of the actual letter William wrote to Dr. James Webb in Cape Fear from his home in Marion:

17 July 1840

My dear Sir,

When I last saw you (in Greensboro) I had no doubt but that I would ere this have remitted some money to pay on my note due the Bank of Cape Fear. I was then on my way to Miss. to dispose of my plantation *and negroes. I made some propositions and rec'd some offers, but did not effect a sale. I went over two weeks since, and carried near $4000 worth of good articles (Watches principally) & have actually offered some at short cost for the sake of raising money but the truth is there is no money in the country. So soon as I make my crop, I expect to sell it all & the land & perhaps the land & negroes together. It is a valuable & saleable place, 400 acres all enclosed & 200 acres in cultivation. I had sold to a young man of that neighborhood one fourth of all I had in the place for $5500 on 1,2,3, or 4 years time, & he to attend to the Farm. He is a fine man & good Manager but owing to my difficulties he generously agreed to recind the trade & manage for me till Christmas next, so that I could make a sale. All my property in this state (except my store house and lot in Greensboro) is conveyed in trust to my creditors to secure them & in view also of my liability as endorser. That case was continued till next Feby owing to the absence of Thomas M. C. Prince, a material witness. Scarcely any one now thinks we (Col Simms & myself) will have to pay that debt. But such has been my mental suffering since last Fall that I have determined to sell all my property and pay all I owe. I rec'd a letter from Bro. Martin before I left home 2 weeks since & one this week urging me & Bro. Jno. to send the money to you that he expected to be sent in August... I also offered my House & Lot in Greensboro (for which 3 years since I was offered $4000) for $1500 cash... but could not effect a sale. Bro John & myself have discharged two Journeymen and have determined to do all the work ourselves. We get as much as we can do, make from 5 to 8 $ per day each. I set out on a travelling tour in a few days to the Springs & Up the Country & will do all the work I can. I made last week $20 and only worked*

3 days in the neighborhood of my place. Now, My Good old friend, in as much as I will most certainly dispose of property sufficient to pay my debts, yet all but just enough to carry on my trade so soon as the Season arrives... I hope you will not, unless the interests of the Bank require it, proceed vs Bro Martin. I will assuredly pay the debt this Fall. Bro Jno is endeavouring to sell his handsome House and Lot to Judge Harris who now lives in one of my Houses, the one I occupied when you were here. I think he can get $5000 for it & he will pay his debt also ... I saw Wm P. Webb at Eutau...We cannot hear anything now but the unceasing discussion of politics. The Whig Electoral ticket is as strong perhaps as any in the Union & they are canvassing the Whole State. I really now think Ala will go for Harrison, in the language of the times, the Whig Cause is "Going Ahead." If you can spare time I will be pleased to receive one of your short letters, should you consent to indulge me a little longer or not, I shall ever feel that I am under Many & Great Obligations to Dr. Webb.

Your assured friend
Wm Huntington 1.

1. *Huntington Silversmiths 1763-1885 pp.87,88*
   William Johnston Hogan 1977

It was quite obvious that all too soon that the business world of the Huntington's would go down like a sinking ship. A sheriff's sale was eventually held in Marion that disposed of all his goods and holdings, plus two valuable lots that once belonged to both William and John Huntington. Soon after this, John took his wife, Salina, and moved to

Pontotoc, Mississippi, in search for a fresh new beginning and the start of his family. Following the birth of their son, John Gray, born in 1841, the couple went on to have five more children: Valeria Rebecca, Desareta, William Martin, Mary Louisa, and another baby daughter, Anlo Huntington.

After his brother John left Alabama, William still went through several business deals that were not very profitable to him. It continued to be like a thorn in his side while he struggled over some of the bad decisions he had made, although he never allowed his mistakes to get him down. Frances never said a word against her husband for all his bad choices. The decision to have all the remaining real estate put into France's name proved to help bring William back from his financial disasters over the next years. Frances seemed to have considerable business sense as William would later give her the credit for helping him come through his struggles.

"After Papa died, I don't know what I would have done had it not been for my dear, Frances," William would always say whenever the thought came to his mind.

William had another issue that was soon to be delivered to him while he continued to keep his family well cared for during the next coming days. The news that Frances would share with him came as no surprise to William while he sat and pulled off his boots on the back porch after coming in from the garden.

"Dr. Reid says the baby should arrive in October," Frances said to her husband who didn't appear to be overjoyed with the news this time.

"Life goes on," he said while he put his arms around his wife and held her close to his side.

Seven months later, William anxiously waited in the parlor while he sat there with his sister, Sarah, and his four boys, Wm Henry, Isaac, Duke, and Martin Palmer, who was about to turn three years old. In the Huntington bedroom, Frances was bearing down while she sat in pain on the birthing chair as Vangie pressed a cool wet cloth to her forehead. Dr. Reid knelt before Frances on the floor while he peered over his wire-framed spectacles, just in time to see the appearance of a baby's head crowned with thick dark hair. Only moments later, with a final push, emerged another healthy baby boy, while the doctor quickly pulled the crying infant from his mother's trembling body. Dr. Reid cut the cord and handed the baby to Delce, who was now present at his side while Vangie helped Frances onto the bed. By the time that Delce got him all cleaned up and wrapped in a clean flannel blanket, Vangie had Frances washed, dressed in a fresh gown, and sitting up in bed to receive her baby boy into her waiting arms.

In the parlor, William said to Sarah, "I think it's going to be a girl this time. I want to name our daughter, Mary Frances, and call her May after my mother."

"Yes, Will," she said, "but what if it's another boy?"

"We already have his name picked out just in case that happens again," he laughed.

The Huntington's seventh son was born on 16 October 1840 and was given the name of William's great-nephew, David Yarbrough. Alas, William Huntington would never have any daughters of his own, but he cherished all his sons while he taught them godly principles and watched them grow up into their teens and beyond.

The Perry County census in June 1850 showed that William Huntington owned nine slaves, whose ages ranged from four years to sixty-five. On the page where the household names and ages were written, the ink had become smeared and the page faded to the point where there was difficulty in reading the fine print. The name of the four year old could not be determined, but there was the names of Delce, Micah, Cassie, and Vangie, which would account for five. At the bottom of the tattered page, torn off after the name beginning West… it had to be assumed that Ariana Weston and Jed Harper had returned to the William Huntington household, and that would bring the count to seven. The final two persons listed as his slaves would remain unknown. There was no mention of a blacksmith shop as William had back in Hillsborough in 1823, but the unknown individuals would have most likely helped him in his shop.

It was during this period and decade that the most tragic events of their lifetime happened rapidly to William and Frances Huntington. William would later write verses and poems to express his personal griefs and losses during those years.

Polly Gale, William's half-sister, passed away in 1839 at the age of 54 in Norwich, Connecticut.

On 6 September 1844, at age fourteen, Duke Howze Huntington died from a distressing disease in Marion.

On 12 October 1850, at age twenty-three, Isaac Howze Huntington died from an unknown illness in Marion.

Martin Palmer, William's brother died in 1851 in Marion at age 54.

On 28 August 1852, at age fifteen, Martin Palmer Huntington died after he drowned while bathing in the tub at the house in Marion.

John Huntington, William's brother, passed away in 1855 in Pontotoc, Mississippi at the age of 47, leaving his wife Salina and six children.

Sarah Huntington Clancy, William's sister, died in 1856 in Marion at the age of 66.

Priscilla Huntington Wallis, William's sister, passed away in 1858 at age 62 in Marion.

Nancy Huntington Hogan, William's sister, also died that same year 1858 at age 58 in Hillsborough, North Carolina.

When the Census of 1860 appeared that June, there was indication that the financial crisis that William had experienced from the 1840's and 1850's had passed. William Huntington was listed as a jeweler, age 68; Frances Howze Huntington, age 58, realtor; and David Yarbrough Huntington, age 21, a clerk living at home with his parents. There was no listing for any slaves or servants, but it is thought that Delce had most likely survived and remained now employed by the family of three while assuming that her children, Micah and Cassie, were grown and living on their own. The other surviving son, William Henry Huntington, had long been gone from home, but never left Marion.

The census reflected at this time the Huntington's real estate was worth $6000 with personal property worth

$7000. William's jewelry shop remained in his house on West Lafayette while he continued to create many artistic pieces of silver during the period before the civil war. There were now three generations of the family, and five gifted artisans who would rise to be known as the Huntington Silversmiths – Roswell, William, Martin Palmer, John, and William Henry.

Many years have passed while the silver pieces produced and simply known as Huntington silver have become scarce, extremely rare, while collections must still survive out there somewhere in the United States, the State of Alabama, Perry County, and Marion. Most likely, a lot of the existing silver had to be hidden away while the North and South were soon to be swept away into the War Between the States. The Civil War was about to begin while Perry County, the town of Marion, and the rest of the state of Alabama, was about to feel the pangs of war and how it would affect everyone who lived during this time. No matter how tragic – *Life goes on ...*

David Yarbrough grew up to become a young man of twenty-one years almost like an only child. Always to remain their baby boy, William and Frances doted on the lad, especially since William Henry had been gone from home for several years. Frances was always knitting him mittens or socks and keeping measurements on him to see how tall he was each passing year. His father, William, showed him Christian ethics, the plan of salvation in the Presbyterian faith by his own example, along with how to treat your fellowman. Also, how to farm, fish, hunt, and shoot a rifle and a shot gun. How he loved that boy, and now to think that in just a few days, he would be heading out on his own. How lonely would it be at home when William and Frances no longer could see his always smiling, handsome face, hear his laugh, his voice, or force a chuckle at his corny jokes. That day had finally arrived.

"Now Mama, you know I have the Lord Jesus in my heart and the love of God for my protection, along with all the prayers from you and Daddy, so please don't worry about me, for Heaven's sakes! And please, don't cry! Always know that I am doing what I want to do, and this is entirely my decision."

Frances dabbed her eyes with her crumpled handkerchief. "I know, Son, it's all for you because we are so proud of you and love you so much. David, you won't realize what a parent feels in a situation like this until you become one yourself."

"Where's Daddy? He told me that he wanted to drive me to Greensboro to meet up with my outfit that will be headed on down to Mobile."

"He'll be here directly, Son. Are you sure you have everything packed in your bag? Do you have those mittens and extra socks I made for you? You know it can get really cold in Mobile during the winter."

"Yes, Mama, no worries. I have everything ready to go, just waiting to see my father."

"I guess he is bringing the buggy around to the front porch," Frances said while she and David left his room.

Private D.Y. Huntington was now an enlisted man in the Confederate Army with orders to serve with the Marion Rifles while stationed at Fort Morgan on the Gulf of Mexico near Mobile, Alabama. William and Frances tried to find consolation in the fact that David would only be about two hundred miles from them, but in a place they had never seen or visited. Maybe at some point, they could plan a trip down south to see him or he might be able to come back home for Christmas. Yes, by all means, that could very well happen.

Frances stood on the porch beside David while they watched William bring the buggy from the back yard, down the tiny access road, and turn onto West Lafayette Street where he stopped the two mule team in front of the house. David picked up his bag, kissed his mother goodbye, and headed down the steps to meet his waiting father. He pitched his bag into the back seat of the buggy and jumped into the front seat beside his father. Looking back as the buggy began to pull away, David threw up his hand in a farewell wave to his mama while Vangie suddenly appeared on the porch to hold onto Frances to help steady her.

"I love you, Son," Frances cried out. "Don't forget to write!"

"I will, Mama, and I love you, too!"

Frances pulled away from Vangie and ran down the front steps and into the street where she watched the buggy travel all the way down to Washington Street until it made the corner and turned. Her boy was gone now from her view, but he would always remain in her heart.

It was early afternoon when William started his return trip home after dropping off his son at the designated meeting place for all the new Confederate recruits leaving Greensboro for Fort Morgan. It was a tough goodbye that had ended with a firm handshake, slap across the back, and a tight manly bear-hug. There would be no tears, but inside William suppressed what he was feeling and that feeling wasn't a good one. The ultimate joy he had once felt for his son on this new venture, had suddenly caused him inward pain and sorrow, but he dared not show it. Not now, not ever while he choked out his last words to his smiling son.

"Well, Father, this is it! Don't you and Mama worry

about me. I will be fine, and I promise to write every chance I get."

"Take care, David, we love you, Son. May the good Lord bless and keep you safe until we see you again."

One final glance while William sat in the buggy, picked up the reins, and gazed into the dark brown eyes of his baby boy, now fully grown into a man. He gave a tug with his shaking hands on the reins and started for home.

In a few weeks, the first letter arrived, and Frances could hardly wait until William closed the shop and came into the house to open and read the letter. They sat together on the sofa in the parlor while they began to read:

21 January 1861

My dear Parents,

It's (the food) some better, as we now have sugar in our coffee... There is a little house outside the Fort where a woman keeps oysters, bread, and coffee... I have heard that this woman will have to leave for selling whiskey to soldiers; when she leaves we will have a hard time getting something to eat ... I understand that money is being subscribed in Marion for our company. I would not advise you to subscribe any for we will not get it; it would be thrown away, if you wish to send me anything, money or provisions, send to me individually ... I would have finished my letter last night, but thought you would rather I would attend church. I did so and heard an excellent sermon from Noble D. Votie. Marius Johnson and myself will go to Mobile tomorrow. We will have our pictures taken in camp life style and sent to you so that you can see what sort of specimens we are.

I have turned out my whiskers now, and I doubt very much whether or not, you will know me... Mrs. Sumter Lea and Miss Mattie Lea came to the Fort yesterday and came into our camp. We all ran to meet them in our blue shirts, and I was so rejoiced at the sight of a woman, that it came near running me crazy. I don't believe I have been in my right senses since. I must stop now to drill with our company ... Love to Bro. Will and family and everybody generally.

Your affectionate son

P.S. You will please take good care of my shot gun. I wrote to Bro. Will a day or two ago.

2. *Huntington Silversmiths 1763 – 1885 pp.106-107*
    William Johnston Hogan 1977
    First letter of David Yarbrough Huntington to his parents from Fort Morgan
    21 January 1861

The next month, William and Frances received a second letter from their son from Fort Morgan. While William had gone uptown to purchase a few supplies, Frances could wait no longer while she sat on the back porch, tore open the envelope, and read the letter:

1 February 1861

My dear Parents,

... as one or two persons will leave this place today for Marion, I embrace the opportunity to thank you for your kind remembrance – I allude to the basket of

provisions "from home" – the same Br. Will and Sister Bert for a box of nice provisions ... I keep well and in good spirits ... so you need not feel the least uneasy about me ... send me all the Marion papers. The boys here fight and fuss over a Marion paper like a dozen hungry hogs would over an ear of corn... I dreamed last night of going home and I thought I saw you all so plainly and this morning I was surprised to find myself half-covered with straw in Fort Morgan, instead of talking with a nice young Lady of my acquaintance now residing in Marion ... Love to everybody.

Your Affectionate Son,
D. Y. Huntington

P.S. Jno Mosely can tell you I am "as fat as a buck" and as tough as a lightwood knot.

3.   *Huntington Silversmiths 1763 – 1885 p. 107*
     William Johnston Hogan 1977
     Second letter of D.Y. Huntington to his parents from Fort Morgan
     1 February 1861

The correspondence between William, Frances, and David continued throughout the rest of the year on a regular basis until the letters from David stopped coming after July 1862. Unknown to them during that time, a select squadron of infantrymen were being activated and ordered to Prince William County, Virginia, during the first week in August to support the Confederate forces already there and gearing up to fight the Second Battle of Bull Run, or as the Confederates called it, the Second Battle of Manassas.

Private David Yarbrough Huntington volunteered to participate in that campaign since he felt it was his expected duty as a soldier. He was an excellent shot with a rifle, but totally green with no fighting experience, whatsoever. Was he scared? Probably. Was he willing to serve? By all means! His father had taught him to stand for what he believed in, so to be able to serve the Confederacy with the Marion Light Infantry, Company G, 4th Alabama Infantry was the foremost thing on his mind.

The Second Battle of Manassas

Following the First Battle of Bull Run, which was fought 21 July 1861, another battle would again be fought on the same former battlefield. The Second Battle of Bull Run (or Second Manassas) took place 29-30 August 1862 between the Army of North Virginia, led by Confederate General Robert E. Lee against the Army of Virginia, commanded by Union Major General John Pope. At this time, while the Confederacy faced off against the Union, this battle would consist of a greater number of men on a much larger scale from the previous encounter of the past year. Private David Yarbrough Huntington, along with his infantrymen from Fort Morgan had been ordered out as a support unit for Lee's army, commanded by Major General James Longstreet. The hot summer during the first week in August found the young twenty-two year old son of William and Frances Huntington, headed off to do battle in Virginia. His only worry now was not having the time to get another letter to his folks to inform them of his call to active duty.

Confederate Major General Thomas J. "Stonewall" Jackson captured the Union supply depot at Manassas Junction, following a wide-range flanking march which cut-off Pope's line of communication with Washington City. Moving on to a new position to the northwest, Jackson concealed his troops in a strong defensive plateau on Stony Ridge to await the arrival of the wing led by Longstreet.

On 28 August, General Jackson attacked a Union column located east of Gainesville at Brawner's Farm, which resulted in a stalemate; however, it successfully got Pope's attention. On that same day, General Longstreet and his men broke through the line of Union resistance in the Battle of Thoroughfare Gap while they made their approach onto the battlefield. This was going to be young David's first encounter with the enemy, while he experienced his first feeling of what it would be like to kill someone, such as a young man, just like himself. Hunting was one thing, but to form a line, and stand there to shoot across a field at a man who was now your enemy, and expect him to fire back in return to kill you, was now no longer just a feeling, but stark reality. Somehow, through God's divine protection, David came through this skirmish without a scratch. Not so, for three of his buddies that had stood shoulder to shoulder with him, and now lay dead on the ground.

Pope convinced himself that he had somehow trapped Jackson, so he concentrated the bulk of his army toward him by the day's end. On 29 August, as the new day began, Pope made a series of assaults against the position Jackson held along an unfinished railroad grade. At noon, Longstreet moved his men from Thoroughfare Gap and positioned them on Jackson's right flank.

As the next day began on 30 August, Pope started his attack, seemingly unaware that Longstreet was on the field. The final element of Longstreet's command, the Division of Major General Richard H. Anderson, had marched seventeen miles to join his troops while they arrived on the battlefield at 3:00 a.m. Exhausted and unfamiliar with the area, Anderson's men were halted on the ridge located east of Groveton. At dawn, the realization that they were now in an isolated position too close to the enemy, Anderson pulled his men from the area. It was Pope's belief that the Confederate army was in retreat, so he directed his entire corps up the Sudley Road and planned to hit the Confederate right flank.

Following an 8:00 a.m. council of war meeting at Pope's headquarters, his officers attempted to convince General Pope to move ahead with caution. But the Confederates were not retreating, but in fact, were hoping to be attacked. General Lee was still waiting for the chance to counterattack Pope with Longstreet's force. Uncertain, however that Pope would actually attack that day, Lee positioned eighteen artillery pieces under Colonel Stephen D. Lee on the high ground located northeast of Brawner's Farm. This new position was ideally situated to bombard the open fields that spread out in front of Jackson's position. The Confederates attempted to strike the first blow, but the Union artillery proved too much for them while their fire power prevailed. After being blasted by so much shellfire, the southern troops withdrew back to the line of the unfinished railroad.

It came about that Lee and Longstreet agreed that the timing was now right for the long-awaited assault in order to force Pope to surrender or be killed to put an end to this terrible battle. Their main focus lay on Henry House Hill, which had been the key terrain during the first battle of Bull Run. If they could capture this location, it would dominate the potential Union line of retreat. Longstreet already knew that he would not be able to form a well-positioned battle line across this rough terrain, so he had to depend solely on the drive and initiative of all his division commanders. While all of this is going on, Pope was back at his headquarters, unknowingly without a clue as to what was happening in the chaos that had erupted to the south of his location.

During the first two hours of the Confederate assault, a new line of defense had been established by the troops already holding that position with their artillery and fire power. They were waiting on the arrival of Longstreet's last fresh troops to aid them. Amid this last group of soldiers in the mix who now joined to take up their position was Private D.Y. Huntington. No time to be nervous or scared, he just stood there while he thought about his father, his mother, and home while he held his position beside the young boy he just met, Private Beau Reynolds from Albany, Georgia.

A remnant of Major General Richard Anderson's Division now took the offensive while they formed a line on Henry House Hill. They held off the final Confederate attack long enough to give the remaining troops time to withdraw across Bull Run Creek to Centreville. At this time, Stonewall Jackson, upon orders from General Lee to support Longstreet, launched an attack to the north of the turnpike at dusk. The attack coincided with Pope's orders to withdraw his troops, located further north of the turnpike, to assist in the Henry House Hill defense. The Confederate force was able to overrun a number of artillery and infantry units with their fierce assault just before the dark of night settled in. By 7:00 p.m. Pope had established a strong defensive line that aligned with the units on Henry House Hill. At approximately 8:00 p.m. he finally ordered a general withdrawal on the turnpike to Centreville. He knew now it was useless to keep on, while he felt ultimate defeat.

Unlike the battle from a year ago, the Union retreat was quiet and orderly following their departure. The Confederates, now weary from all the fighting and low on ammunition, did not attempt to pursue them in the darkness. Although General Robert E. Lee had won the victory, it was bittersweet for him since he had not achieved his objective of completely destroying Pope's Army. However, success in this battle would empower him in the near future when he set his sights on the Maryland Campaign.

Casualties and losses for the Army of Virginia (Pope) 77,000 est.

14,462 total – 1,747 killed; 8,452 wounded; 4,263 captured/missing

Casualties and losses for the Army of Northern Virginia (Lee) 55,000 est.

7,298 total – 1,096 killed; 6,202 wounded

The Second Battle of Bull Run, like the First, was a significant victory to the Confederacy while it struck a blow to Union morale. Pope was relieved of his command on 12 September 1862, while his army was merged into the Army of the Potomac while it marched into Maryland under the command of General George McClellan. John Pope spent the remainder of the war in the Department of the Northwest in Minnesota while his office dealt with the Dakota War of 1862.

Early in the morning of the next day, the last day of August, the remaining infantrymen from Fort Morgan had assembled themselves once again on the battlefield in the place where they had stood to fight the previous day. While they were grouped together now and standing under a big oak tree, their view was focused on the carnage scattered all over the field, almost as far as they could see. While the buzzards began to circle overhead, their task was to search for all their dead, and possibly those left wounded and dying. Following a silent prayer, the sergeant dismissed his men while they took to the field to begin the search. When the sergeant was satisfied that enough time had been given, at mid-morning he ordered that the search would end. A one horse drawn wagon had already been dispatched to the scene in the event of survivors, but mainly for the dead. There was only a small yield as the five dead were loaded onto the wagon bed while the only wounded man they found was placed on the seat beside the driver. While the wagon prepared to leave the area, the sergeant and the rest of the small band fell in to walk out behind the wagon. As the entourage began to move slowly around several bodies that remained in the path to the road, the wounded man began to shout and point over to a place nearby toward a patch of tall grass. The sergeant suddenly halted the wagon and immediately left his men while he quickly made his way over to take a look at what the man had just pointed out to him.

Laying there in the grass, side by side, the sergeant observed the two young men, one face up and one face down. He did not recognize the deceased blond soldier whose once blue eyes staring back at him now appeared so very dull. He reached into the lad's pockets to check for any identification and pulled out his papers. He found him to be Private Beau Reynolds from Albany, Georgia. The sergeant motioned for two of the boys behind the wagon to come take his body away while he slowly turned the body of the dark haired boy over on the ground. He was about to check this unfortunate whiskered young man, who appeared to be in his early twenties, for identification. At first sight, there was no need for this because the sergeant immediately recognized this young man as one of his own from Fort Morgan. With a look of peace on his face, there on the ground lay Private David Yarbrough Huntington, shot through the head.

When the news of David's death finally reached his parents, William would no longer say ever again "Life goes on" because his world just ended. William and Frances were crushed and completely devastated over this tragic event that stayed with them for the rest of their lives.

Arrangements were made by Headquarters at Fort Morgan and the Confederate government to have the body transported by rail from Virginia to Selma, Alabama.

William would be waiting on that day at the train station to finally take his boy home to Marion.

Chapter 8

William Huntington was seventy years old on that brisk September day in 1862 while he and Frances stood close together at the gravesite of their beloved David Yarbrough. Now, five of their sons were at rest together in the Huntington family plot, along with William's father, Roswell. The autumn leaves were beginning to fall all around in the Marion Cemetery while William held onto Frances to guide her toward the buggy where William H. stood waiting to drive them home. All of David's letters that Frances kept in her dresser drawer would become the way she could cherish the memory of her soldier boy, while she would read them over and over on the days she felt really sad and depressed. After having seven sons, William Henry was the Huntington's only living heir, now a man who had recently turned thirty-nine. He would soon become the main concern for his aging parents, while William Henry was heard to say, "Life goes on ..."

Following the death of his brother, William Henry

gained an entirely new perspective on what the civil war and its effect was having on the town of Marion, his friends, and now his family. It was hard to shake the feelings he had about the loss of David, but what could he do? He wanted to serve his country like his baby brother, but he could never put his parents, his wife, and children through anything like what the family had just experienced. As the only surviving son, he knew it would absolutely kill his mother and father should anything happen to him right away. Then, he had an idea that suddenly popped into his head.

After several jobs that he had worked locally after finishing school and throughout his youth, William Henry worked alongside his father while they continued at this time producing even more unique silver pieces. Wm Henry would come to the house on West Lafayette three days during the week where he would help polish the silver that William would make in his shop at home during his absence. The weekend was coming up, so William Henry decided it was time to share with his father what was weighing so heavily on his heart and mind. He had already shared his feelings with his wife, so he was relieved that she accepted what he had to tell her, and that made it easier for him to now approach his still grieving father.

It was late Friday afternoon, while William was putting up the last of the tools and taking off his apron that William H. approached him as he was about to leave the shop.

"Daddy, do you have a few minutes before you go that we could talk?"

"Certainly, Son, what's bothering you? I could already tell by watching you today that you must have something really troubling you. You seemed to be in a daze for most of the day."

"Yes sir, I guess I have so I'll just get to the point where I can get this off my chest if you don't mind."

"Let's hear it, Son. Do I need to sit down?"

"If you prefer, that's fine. Yes, let's both sit down. Please tell me how you feel about what I'm planning to do."

"Henry, you know your mother and I stand by to support practically anything you, Elizabeth, and the girls want to do. I'm listening, Son."

"At thirty-nine, taking into consideration all that's happened in our family, I feel I want to serve in the Confederate army for the war effort and to honor the memory of David Yarbrough who willingly gave his life for his country by my joining the Home Guard here in Marion. In that way, I will be able to fulfill my desire to serve while I continue to work here with you and for you. What do you think about that?"

"I'm not all that familiar with the home guard, as you say. Tell me about it. Is this going to upset your mother? If it does, then I won't hear another word about it, do you understand?"

"Yes sir, but let me …just hear me out and then you can decide the best way to approach her where I may receive her complete approval."

"I would be enlisting as a private in Porter King's Perry County Militia Home Guard CSA. Most of the Confederate home guard units work closely with the Confederate Army for the defense of the home front. Here at home, in our case, it would be Marion, Perry Ridge, Heiberger, and basically all the other towns located in and around Perry County. Our unit would also be responsible for tracking down and capturing any or all Confederate army deserters in the area."

"Will you receive pay for your service?" William asked.

"No sir, the home guard is strictly made up from volunteers that will not receive a salary; however, a bounty may be offered in some cases by the Confederate government for the capture of certain wanted deserters. Now, I've heard more recently that due to all the mounting debt, it is becoming rare that a bounty is paid. It all depends, I guess."

"Will you be issued a uniform?"

"No, there is no uniform, just regular clothing, but the men should make an effort to wear the same color as the Confederate soldiers."

"I see," said William. "Tell me more, and convince me that this is really what you want to do."

For the next few minutes, William Henry went into complete detail by telling his father everything he had come to know about the home guard. He knew he had to really convince his mother and father about his enlistment and meet their approval; otherwise, this was never going to happen for him in a very pleasant manner.

Home guard units are basically set up to be a last defense against any possible invading Union forces. They also try to gather information about Union troop movements in the area, as well as to identify and control any local civilians who may be considered sympathetic to the union cause. The men receive no military training, but they could possibly be drafted into the Confederate forces should the need suddenly arise. The home guard is simply recognized as a service to the Confederacy, and is usually made up from older men or others that have been exempted from front line service in the army.

Depending on the area of the county, Porter King's Militia Home Guard would most of the time be nothing more than a group of men working from home as they pleased. Several home guard units have base camps and headquarters, ride on patrol, and scout for possible deserters or Union smugglers. Their foremost task is to seek out any soldier that pass through the Confederate battle lines into southern territory and capture any deserters that try to return to their homes. The deserters that are encountered by home guard patrols are dealt with in different fashions. At times, a man will be returned to his army post by a Confederate unit stationed near the area where the deserter is captured. In some cases, deserters are executed by the home guard.

"Well, let's have it, sir. What do you say?" William H. asked his father.

"Son, only you know what you truly want to do. If you and Elizabeth are in complete agreement over this, I don't see how your mother and I can stand in your way. That decision is yours completely as I give you my blessing. May God always be your guide and grant you peace, Henry."

William Henry left his father that day feeling much better.

Now about to reach the age of forty, William Henry was no longer that lean, skinny boy of his youth. His almost six foot frame had filled out quite well through the years while he now possessed a rather stocky build. He had a ruddy complexion, dark hair like his father, which he kept cut to a medium length, and dark brown eyes. He wore no beard, goatee, or moustache, and was always clean shaven ever since the day he married his first love, Elizabeth Reynolds from Marion when she was twenty-four.

William H., now called Henry by his loving wife, Elizabeth, was the father of two daughters. His oldest was named Frances, who was born in 1851 and was now eleven, and Irene, born in 1853, who was nine. Like his parents, Henry and Elizabeth also suffered the loss of a child when their son, born in 1858, suddenly died at five months during the next year. Infant Reynolds Huntington was laid to rest in the Huntington family plot in the Marion Cemetery in 1859, alongside his unknown great-grandfather and five uncles.

Following the aftermath of the Second Battle of Manassas while General Robert E. Lee was marching his troops on to the Maryland Campaign, there were a lot of shaken men who had simply had enough of this war. They had enlisted in a fight they felt would soon be over while they had honored their commitment, and by the grace of God, had survived this horrible battle which had taken so many lives on both sides. Now, with no end to the war in sight, and months and years left in their enlistment as a Confederate soldier, there was only three choices for them to consider.

A man could remain in the service, and most likely come home in a pine box; or be left to rot on some distant battlefield; or buried there in an unmarked grave; or simply be blown to bits by a blast from a heavy mortar shell that would render his body parts scattered in pieces and left on the field for the vultures to eat. Now, that was just the first choice.

The second choice would be to continue to follow orders and march with the troops headed to what was beginning to look like a little town in Maryland called Antietam.

The third, and final choice was simply to tuck tail and run, knowing that to desert meant if caught, to be returned to your company, suffering the pangs of disgrace, dishonor, and maybe a firing squad. So, it came about that many of these daring men who refused no longer to fight, turned their eyes toward home to Tennessee, Georgia, Alabama, and Mississippi, fully knowing what would happen to them if and when they were captured on the run. Those men would now be known as "deserters" while finding them would be the ultimate task for all the local home guards in each state and county. Now, it would become like playing a game of cat and mouse, or running the gauntlet, except now many lives would be at stake, and the final result could only end in a life or death situation.

Private William Henry Huntington of the Porter King Militia Home Guard C.S.A. had only been serving Perry County four months when he encountered his first deserter. It was almost dusk on 14 January 1863 while he and Pvt. John Brennan were riding patrol out close to Heiberger. John and Henry had only met since joining the home guard, so neither of them knew each other very well.

John Lewis Brennan lived on his farm located north of Perry Ridge. John, now at age forty-five, was a tall, burly man, single, who had been a farmer all his life. He was the father of a young son and daughter by two different women. John had a muscular build from working all his years in the field and around the farm. He wore his sandy blond hair cut to a medium length with a goatee and small moustache and had green eyes. A small scar ran down his cheek on the left side of his face that he received at age nineteen in a bar room brawl in Perry Ridge. He was tanned from working in the fields, which provided his deep bronze complexion. His large hands were rough and calloused. His face would never be considered as handsome, but overall, he made his appearance as only average in looks. He rarely smiled, but when he did, his teeth had yellowed from all the years he had smoked tobacco. His voice was low-pitched, gruff, and raspy, most likely from smoking all the time.

Henry had never worked with John before, so they passed their time on horseback in mutual conversation to get more acquainted while they had pulled duty today with each other for the first time. There was never a precise structure for a guard on duty. There could be as many as five men working together on patrol or down to only two. Although a man could be alone in a certain situation while encountering a take-down, it was preferred to work at least in pairs. In that way, there would be additional help when needed, and also provide a witness to what actually happened during an encounter with a known deserter.

Henry and John pulled their mounts to a halt as they observed the sun while it began to disappear below the tree line that lay on the mountainside just ahead. By the time they reached the first sight of the church yard, the two privates decided to pull up to the front porch of the Heiberger Methodist Church and camp there until early morning. The dark of night was about to settle in and they would only have the moonlight to guide them back to Marion if they chose to leave now.

"Did you see that?" John said in a low voice while they both pulled their horses to a sudden stop as they were about to turn onto the church yard.

"See what?"

"I thought I saw a flame around back of the church, and now it is out. I swear it was a flash that lit up for a few seconds."

"No, I didn't see anything, John. Maybe it was a shooting star."

"Now, dammit, I smell smoke! Somebody's had a fire going around back, and whoever it is has probably seen us already. We need to check it out," John said while he started to move out in that direction.

Henry and John rode on down to the church, dismounted, and tied both horses to one of the posts on the front porch. After drawing their revolvers, the two began to creep down the side of the building while they moved suspiciously toward the rear of the little white church house. As they rounded the corner, up close to the back door, Henry and John could see a few of the embers from the almost extinguished campfire still glowing there on the ground. It was almost dark, and there were no signs of anyone around back, but someone was nearby because the fire didn't just start by itself. John walked to the door and pulled on the latch to check, and the door was locked. On the ground, near the fire, Henry pointed out to John that it looked as if someone had been laying on the ground very close to the fire. The grass had been pressed down in that area and both Henry and John sniffed in the air like they could almost smell the body odor of a weary traveler nearby.

"You might as well come on out! We know you're hiding under the church house," Henry yelled out while he looked down at the crawlspace.

"Hey, my friend, your smell gives you away, and this damn fire didn't just put itself out," John shouted.

"Are you hurt or hungry? Maybe we can help, if you will show yourself and come out from under there. We know you are there, son," Henry said while he motioned to John, who now stood a bit closer to the opening.

Click!

"Don't think I didn't hear that! Throw your weapon out as you crawl from where you are right now. We just want to talk," John said.

"We're not leaving, so I'm about to get your fire started back up after I gather a few sticks and twigs. We will just camp out here for the rest of the night, and you can remain under the church in the cold. It's your choice," said Pvt. Huntington while he called out in a loud voice in the dark.

While Henry was gathering anything he could find to throw onto the fire, John saw the end of a Spencer rifle suddenly appear while it slowly slid out from under the church building. He quickly grabbed onto the end of the barrel and pulled with a yank while it released from the hands that had held it. From underneath the floor crawled a scared, young Confederate soldier.

As the young lad stood to his feet, the rank smell of body odor rapidly mixed with the night air while the strong scent slowly faded away somewhat. The boy appeared unshaven with at least a week old beard, and his deep blue eyes looked tired and bloodshot. His face and hands were dirty and he wore a soiled Confederate uniform with no kepi, only his bare head with long, stringy coal black hair. He stood about 5' 10", and had a medium build. He probably weighed about 165 pounds and appeared to be very tired and hungry. He would most likely have been a handsome young man, had he been given a chance to shave, bathe, and dress in a fresh, clean uniform. Now, he felt like a grizzly bear caught in a trap. All he could do now was to throw himself on the mercy of his two captors and pray.

"Please, don't shoot, I'm comin' out," he pleaded.

"Well, what have we here? I know, son, you're probably just lost from your company and trying to find them so that you can get back before they miss you, huh?" asked Pvt. Brennan.

"Naw, I can't say that, mister," said the trembling young man standing there while he looked at his interrogator in the dark.

"Well, boy, what do you say? Sit yore young ass down and pray tell me what you're doin' in these parts. I really don't believe we have any regular army from your company stationed anywhere here in the county. Better still, just wait until my partner gets back 'cause he'll want to hear what you've got to say."

Moments later, Henry returned and threw an armload of sticks and twigs onto the smoldering fire. He bent down to blow and poke at the fire until a small flicker appeared to ignite the flame as the fire began to slowly catch up and burn. He looked across at the young soldier sitting there by the fire.

"Whoa, John, whose this we have here?"

"We gotta lost soldier here, I'm afraid, just hankering to tell us what the hell he's doin' here in Perry County."

"Who are you, son, and where are you headed?" Henry asked the lad.

"I'm Pvt. Michael Channing, and I'm trying to get back to my home in Jackson, Mississippi to my parent's house. I have been on the move for several days now, and I'm tired and hungry."

"Sorry, but we don't have nothin' to eat, but if you're still with us in the morning, we can probably get you somethin' to eat," John said.

"Where's your company now?" Henry asked while he took a seat on the ground beside John Brennan.

"I have no idea, but the last I heard my sergeant say was that Company B, 5th Mississippi Infantry would soon be on the march to Antietam."

"Is that a fact?" Pvt. Brennan asked. "So, you're thinkin' now, those orders don't apply to me, so I'll just turn around and head south back to my home. Is that about right, Private Channing?"

"Guess I've had about enough, no more fighting for me! I've got a girl back home, and I don't want to end up dead in Antietam. This war is terrible!"

"How old are you, Pvt. Channing?" Henry asked.

"Nineteen, I'll be twenty in April."

"Nineteen, huh? Well, young man, this is what is about to happen. My name is Pvt. Henry Huntington, and the man seated on my left is Pvt. John Brennan, and we are a patrol unit for the Porter King Militia Home Guard of Perry County. If you don't know it, son, that is the county you are in right now. It is our duty to capture any Confederate deserters, whoever they may be, and arrange to have them transported back to their company or division for sentencing. So, what then are we going to do with you? In the morning, you'll be taken to our headquarters not far from here. Arrangements will be made at that time to return you to Company B, 5th Mississippi."

"Please, you can't do that! I beg you to let me go. I've just got to get home as soon as I can. I'll leave here this very moment if you'll just let me. Please, I'm begging, don't send me back," the young private pleaded.

"If we do that, son, we'll not be doing the job that's expected of us," John said. "Just why in the hell do you think that the Home Guard, entirely supported by the C.S.A. was created in the first place?"

"All I know, Pvt. Brennan, is that I can't go back, and I can be home in two or three more days. Please, again I beg you, just let me go!"

"I'm afraid that's pretty much impossible, Pvt. Channing. You see, you happen to be our prisoner now, and the two of us will be taking you in at sun up in the morning. You might as well forget about going home anytime soon," John said.

The boy almost cried, but held back any visible sign of a tear. "Then, I'm as good as dead!"

"No son, you're not," said Henry. "When you go back to your camp, you could possibly get a few lashes, time in the stockade, a cursing out by your commander, or a dishonorable discharge, but you could survive that. You appear to me to be strong and healthy, only a bit smelly right now 'cause you do stink, but at least you would be alive to eventually return home. We need to…"

"Yes, I know," said Pvt. Brennan while he got up and left to go check on the horses. When he returned in a few minutes, in his hand he carried some short pieces of rope. "Here's what we're going to do now. Everyone's going to walk over to that bush and relieve themselves, and then come back around the fire and bed down for the night. Private Channing, you will have your hands and feet bound with this rope until morning. All right, gentlemen, let's do it while remembering that I will have my revolver ready to shoot, just in case somebody decides they want to make a run for it," John said.

As the three men began to settle down around the fire, Henry was the last one down since he found a few more sticks of wood to build up the fire for the rest of the night. He threw them on, the fire blazed up, and Henry settled down on the spot he had chosen next to Private Channing.

"I'll take first watch, if you want," he said.

"That's fine with me," said John. "Wake me whenever you get ready for me to take over."

Late evening or night patrols always carried a bed roll on their mounts to have in situations like this. It was fortunate that Henry had an extra blanket which he threw over the young soldier. Henry lay where he could keep a watchful eye out for the young man for most of the night while he thought about how they would transport Private Michael Channing to their headquarters in the morning. Pvt. Channing lay awake for a long time before he eventually went to sleep after he kept thinking of ways to make his escape. John Brennan, who now lay sleeping and snoring, had already thought about what he was planning since the moment he first saw the young deserter crawl out from under the church house. If his plan worked, well, he would just have to wait and see.

It had to have been some time after midnight when Henry woke up his partner, John, to take over the watch. Their prisoner had moved very little since he was tightly bound, and laying fast asleep on the cold ground. Henry went to find more fuel for the fire. He returned with a couple of small logs which he threw on the fire before he lay down finally to try to get some sleep.

At sunrise, John stood and went around to where Henry was sleeping to awaken him. Seeing that their prisoner was still asleep, they both went back to take care of business behind the bush. On their return, John kicked Channing on a boot that was sticking out from under his blanket.

"Wake your ass up, Private. I know that we're all hungry, so let's get a move on it this frosty morn," John ordered his captive. "Hopefully, we can get some breakfast at headquarters when we all get there."

"Sounds good to me, but I'm probably not as hungry as Pvt. Channing, am I right?" Henry asked while looking down at the boy. There was no comment from him while the young private lay there with his eyes open, but not saying anything. John walked back over and kicked him harder this time.

"My partner just asked if you were hungry. Answer him!" John shouted.

"Yes, I'm hungry, but now I need to relieve myself. How about removing these ropes and letting me go? I'm not going anywhere."

John quickly spoke up once again while he looked directly at Henry. "Why don't you take the blankets, after we roll them up, around to the front and get the horses ready. Channing, here can ride on the back of my horse with me. If that doesn't work, then the bastard will just have to walk, while I'm sure his young ass is used to that by now. I'll cut him loose, where he can take care of business, and when I see the fire is completely out, we'll be on around to the front to join you. Just wait there for us."

It seemed to Henry that there had been ample time for John to finish up around back while he re-tied the horses to the post. He decided to go check to see what was keeping them so long. All of a sudden, in the quietness of the early morning, two shots rang out that had to come from John's weapon alone. Channing's rifle had already been secured across Henry's saddlebag, while his own revolver was holstered at his side. What just happened behind the church? Henry immediately broke into a run. When he made the corner of the building, he saw John, clutching the revolver in his right hand, standing over Michael Channing, while the young private lay face down. Blood now began to ooze from his nose and mouth while it poured onto the ground.

He lay there still and motionless as John put his weapon back into the holster.

"You killed him!" Henry exclaimed. "Why…what just happened?"

"While I was fastening my britches, the fool just took off to run. I yelled to him to stop or I'll shoot. He never turned back, and I barely had time to pull my revolver out after I had warned him."

"You could have gone after him, tackled him, and put him down on the ground without just shooting him in the back. Why wouldn't you have done that?" Henry questioned.

"I swear, it all just happened so fast, and I wasn't thinking. It was only a quick reflex and I didn't…"

"Now, what are we going to do?"

"Well, Henry, you know the Home Guard can bring a deserter in, dead or alive. I say, we go back to headquarters, file a report, fetch a wagon, and take the boy in and try to collect a bounty for him. After Porter King hears my story, and I put in the request to the C.S.A. office in Montgomery, then I may be entitled to collect the bounty. I'll split my share with you, if you say that you witnessed everything that happened just like I already told you."

"I didn't see a damn thing, John! What makes you think I could support anything you have to say as the absolute truth? That would be a boldface lie right from the beginning, no way, man. For all I know, you could have shot this poor boy on purpose."

"You accusing me of intentionally doing this deed to a known deserter, like I just up and murdered him? Sure, I shot the bastard, but it was an accident. An accident, you hear!

I was in pursuit of a Confederate deserter who was trying to escape and after firing a warning shot, I attempted to wound him, but my shots proved fatal. I'm sorry!"

"After this is cleared, I want no more dealings with you, John Brennan, or your bounty, should you even get one. I hope to never ride another patrol with you. I would just quit the guard if that were to happen."

"Well, Henry…"

"Just stop, and let me finish! Accident or not, things just don't add up, John. First, I never heard you yell out the warning, and secondly, Pvt. Channing fell no further than five or six feet from the bush where you said you both had been standing when he decided to run. That boy never had a chance, did he? You don't have to answer that since we both already know. Dammit! Let's go get the wagon, John, I'm ready to get this over and done with."

"You can believe what you want, Henry Huntington, but I know in my heart what really happened, and I will testify and swear under oath on a Bible, that it was entirely accidental just like I told you, my friend. I deeply regret this, and I am truly sorry for my actions."

That morning, Pvt. Michael Channing finally got to go home, but it wasn't Mississippi like he had planned.

Chapter 9

William Henry Huntington continued to work in the shop with his father while putting in all the extra hours he could manage to help out, since William had somewhat slowed down his production during the past several months. The two of them together had created so many fine pieces over the past year, and sales were doing well. It seemed that there was hardly a household in Marion that did not possess a piece or collection of fine Huntington silver. Due to the fact that his father was now getting older, William Henry did his best to help encourage his father to keep making and selling his silverware. Nowadays, William went into his shop to work on a piece to have something to occupy his time, rather than trying to profit from sales, since he had already made his fortune and was now living quite well.

Henry remained in service with the home guard for the next eighteen months. During that time, he had experienced a number of take-downs of captured deserters, twenty-seven to be exact, but none like the one he encountered with Pvt.

John Brennan, almost a year and a half ago. Although every case is different, the overall results of Henry's cases ended with his captives being safely returned and unharmed to their individual companies. Any punishments would then come from the company commanders, and Henry would never know the outcome. It was only his primary job to locate and find the deserters.

By chance, one day he was called in to his headquarters in Perry Ridge to clear up some paperwork on a recent capture and take-down. While Henry was going through some of the files, one in particular surfaced on the top of the stack he was moving about on the desk. The label on the folder read: *Pvt. John Lewis Brennan – Serial # 127824.* Henry picked it up, opened to the first document, and decided to take a quick look while no one sitting close to him was watching or even looking his way at the time. When he got to page five, he stopped. He could hardly believe what he was seeing, while he re-read that page two more times before quickly closing the file, and shuffling it back into the stack.

The document on page five confirmed what he had suspected all along. There it was, printed in bold black ink, a complete list of every take-down that Pvt. Brennan had participated in that included: the date; the time; the place; rank and name of the deserter; and the most telling of all, the amount of any bounty applied for and collected. William H. had just read the entry he was quickly scanning to confirm his suspicion about Private Brennan. He read: *14 January 1863; abt. 6 pm; Heiberger, Perry County, Alabama;*

Pvt. Michael Channing, Company B, 5th Miss. Infantry;
Bounty collected – 57 dollars.

Henry went on to read quickly through the list to
find any other entries that listed a bounty that had been
collected. He counted a total of eight in a period of nearly
two years, but had no time to add up the total amount
collected from all the dead victims. Henry left the room
that day feeling that every man has to account for all the
deeds he has ever done, whether good or bad. John Brennan
would certainly have to live with everything he had done,
as well as Henry, himself, so he just put it behind him in
his mind and walked out the door while he headed back
home to Elizabeth and his girls. Thank God he didn't have
to work anymore with the likes of John Brennan or anyone
else like him for that matter. Henry quit the home guard
that day and he felt good about it.

Things were slowing down as far as building and
construction was concerned because of the war. Supplies
were getting hard to come by, and many men had enlisted
in the Confederate Army, and were simply gone. The
Huntington's next door neighbors, Napoleon and Mary
Lockett, had stopped construction on the new front porch
they were adding across the entire front of their house.
William and Frances had known them since 1840 when the
Lockett's were first starting to build their house.

Over the years, the Huntington's and Lockett's developed
a cordial relationship as good friends and neighbors, since
the property joined between their two houses. Napoleon
and Mary Lockett were both born and reared in Powhatan
County, Virginia, in 1813 and 1814, respectively. In 1834,

twenty-one year old, Nape, married his twenty year old cousin, Mary Clay Lockett in Virginia. (Mary's father was the youngest brother of Napoleon's father).

While later moving to Marion, they built their house on West Lafayette and settled there to start a family. Nape Lockett was an attorney in Marion, while Mary became a homemaker and mother to their three sons at the time: Powhatan, born in 1836; Samuel Henry, born in 1837; and William Albert, born in 1839.

On this particular day, Frances sat her dresser in the bedroom while she brushed and pinned up her hair, applied a hint of rouge to her cheeks, and lightly powdered her face and neck. She was already dressed in one of her favorite taffeta gowns, which she only wore on special occasions. She deemed the bright royal blue color and the neckline of the dress alone would not be very appropriate to wear to church on Sundays; however, it was perfect for the invitation to tea next door at Mary Lockett's at two o'clock. After she placed her white lace caplet on her head and tied the sash under her chin, she was ready to walk next door to have tea, and hopefully catch up on all the local gossip. William was working in his shop, and she knew that Nape Lockett would most likely be at his office in town, so Frances was looking forward to having tea with Mary, who appeared to her as being in the family way once again.

Frances had been instructed to arrive and come into the house at the west side entrance, since the front portico was in such a mess from the ongoing construction project. As she made her way across the back lawn, Frances walked through the port-cochere' and up the stairs to reach the door.

She gently rapped on the door, and it opened momentarily to reveal a very much pregnant lady, dressed in a billowy green muslin, high-waist gown that fell to ankle length.

"Good afternoon, Frances. I'm glad you were able to come. Isn't it a beautiful day outside? And my, just look at you, so lovely!"

"Thank you, Mary, and you as well, my dear. I love your dress, and now that I see you up close, my suspicions have suddenly ended."

"Come on in, and we'll go into the front parlor to sit. So, you didn't know that I was pregnant again?"

"Not really, but recently I saw you out in the back yard, and I told my husband that I thought you looked like you were going to have another baby."

"Nape is pleased, and he told me that he would like a house full of young un's. Me, I don't know so much about that! Have a seat, Frances, on the sofa if you prefer."

"You both have a lovely home here, but I guess you miss living in Virginia at times when you think about home."

"Thank you, Frances. As you can see, our front porch is a mess, but with the war and everything, it has become rather difficult to finish it. So, I just call it a work in progress."

"The new porch will be a nice addition. I'm sure you will enjoy it once it's finished."

"Yes, I do miss living in Virginia, but this has been our home for a while, and I do love it here in Marion. I want to apologize to you about our tea time. Verna Mae took ill just this afternoon, so I've given her the afternoon off, and she is resting in her room. I have attempted to make the tea cakes myself, and have yet to sample the tea, so we'll see how that turns out to be in a few minutes."

"That is quite all right, Mary. As you may know, Delce does most all our cooking, but lately I have been doing a lot myself since now it's only William and myself. When I had all my boys at home, Delce was a tremendous help to me. I hardly know what I would have done without her."

"That's so true, I do declare. It's hard to get good help nowadays."

"How long have you had Verna Mae?"

"Napoleon bought her for me not long after this house was finished. Since our place here is so much larger than our home in Virginia, he thought she would be a good help for me, and he was right. I'm just like what you said a moment ago, I don't think I could do without her. Verna Mae is a very pleasant girl, so happy and cheerful all the time. I'm sorry she's taken ill."

"I feel the same about Delce, and she's got two children to look after all the time."

"Frances, if you will excuse me for a few minutes, I need to go out to the kitchen and finish preparing our tray. I have everything almost ready, just need to re-heat the tea. Please, make yourself comfortable, and I will return shortly."

While Mary was gone outside to the kitchen, Frances stood and walked across the room to get a closer look at Mary's three sons, whose portraits were hanging on the wall. She didn't know which boys were Powhatan or Albert, but she recognized Samuel in his Confederate uniform. They were such nice looking young men, and their portraits were so realistic, so lifelike. Then she turned toward the beautifully crafted fireplace and gazed up at the portrait of Napoleon Lockett hanging there above the mantelpiece. It was a rather large oil painting, framed in gold leaf, and signed at the bottom right with the name of Nicola Marschall. Frances thought it was a good likeness of Mary's husband, and she was quite impressed with the painting. She had heard about Mr. Marschall and his portrait studio in Marion, but she was unfamiliar with his work. As she returned to her seat, Frances passed close to Mary's chair where her sewing basket sat on the floor with scraps of red and blue material tossed within the basket, along with a swatch of what appeared to be white silk or a similar fabric. Interesting, she thought that this must be the leftover material from when Mary and several other women stitched the new Confederate flag. The very same one that was flown over the state capitol in Montgomery on 4 March 1861.

"Here we go, dear, sorry I took so long," Mary said while she entered and placed the tray with her silver teapot, sugar bowl, two china cups and saucers, and tea cakes on the mahogany table that sat low in front of the sofa.

"What a nice silver service you have, Mary. I don't believe I recognize the unique design. Where did you get it, if I may ask?"

"My dear husband bought it for one of my birthdays a few years back when we lived in Virginia. I believe the silversmith was named Lemuel Lynch, as I recall."

"You don't say! What a surprise that you have just mentioned that to me. We both knew Lemuel from when we lived in Hillsborough and have thought of him many times over the years. At one time, William and Lemuel had a brief partnership, and later, Will sold all his melting equipment to him. He taught Lem everything he needed to know about working with silver."

"That is surprising, Frances, and you will certainly have to tell your husband."

"Don't worry, I shall indeed. He will be also glad to know that Lemuel is probably now living in Virginia."

"Well then, Frances, do you recognize the spoons on the tray beside the teacups?"

She laughed. "Honey, I would know who made those if they were ten feet away. Those spoons were made by none other than Roswell and William Huntington."

"You are quite correct, Frances, and I just love my Huntington silver. In my sideboard in the dining room, I have four knives, forks, and spoons, and also two serving spoons and a ladle. Nape has promised to get me two more place settings one day to finish out my set. That would make a nice Christmas gift, don't you think?"

"I have so much silver, I don't know what to do with all of it!"

"I envy you, Frances. I imagine anything you need or want in silver or jewelry, you just have to tell your husband, and he would make it for you, right?"

"I don't ask him for much. He works hard, and I would rather him make everything to sell. I worry about him so much now. Some days, he won't go to the shop, but I try to encourage him. He sits around and writes poems and verses sometimes when he gets in these moods. We both have our days, and nights especially when we find ourselves down and distressed. We still struggle over the loss of our David.

Look at me, going on like this! Please tell me more about Nicola Marschall and how the making of the new flag all came about."

"My dear Frances, you and William continue to have our deepest sympathy in the loss of your precious son. I can't imagine what it's like for you both. I worry about our second son, Samuel, who is the chief engineer with the Second Regiment, Confederate Engineer Corps, on his way soon to Vicksburg. All we can do is pray for him and that this war will soon end and all our soldiers may be able to return home safely."

"Some things, we will probably never know or understand. We both thought David was still serving at Fort Morgan in Mobile, and never dreamed that he and the Marion Rifles would be ordered to the Second Battle of Bull Run. I'm sorry, Mary, I can't talk about this anymore. Again, please tell me about Mr. Marschall. From what I understand, he is quite an impressive young man, so handsome and debonair!"

"Let me pour you a cup of tea, and I'll tell you all you want to know about him. Have a tea cake, if you dare!"

Frances took her cup, added a spoonful of sugar, and made herself comfortable on the red velvet sofa, while Mary did the same and was then seated in her chair across the room.

"Where do I begin, Frances? There's so much to tell about Nicci, as many of his closest friends call him. Nicola Marschall was born 16 March 1829 in St. Wendel, Germany, to a Prussian family of tobacco merchants. In 1849, he immigrated to America and landed in the port of New

Orleans, but eventually settled in Mobile, Alabama for about a year and a half. In 1851, Nicci re-located to Marion, where he taught Art in his first portrait studio. Not long after that, he was hired as the Art instructor at the Marion Female Seminary for a number of years. It was during that time when Napoleon and I first met him at his first art exhibition at the Seminary."

"Did he continue to work also in his studio?"

"Oh yes, dear, he painted Napoleon's portrait there over the mantel as well as many others including Nathan Bedford Forrest, General Isham Warren Garrott, and Andrew Barry Moore, the Governor of Alabama. It just so happens that the Governor is Powhatan and Albert's father-in-law. My boys married his daughters, Martha and Annie. On a visit one day to Marion to see his daughters, he told them that no flag had been adopted as yet by the Confederate government, and he was planning to hold a competition to seek a design for the flag. Well, after I found out about this, I knew of one man whom I knew could possibly do this. I approached Nicci one day and urged him to submit a design to the governor. His design was chosen, and I was later given the honor, along with several other ladies, to sew the new flag in this very room right where I am sitting now."

"That's wonderful, Mary!"

"Oh, but that's not all, Frances. He was also given credit for the design of the grey Confederate uniform of the soldiers."

"I should like very much to meet this man one day," said Frances.

"Maybe that can be arranged, but now he is presently

serving in the Second Regiment of Confederate Engineers in Vicksburg under our son, Major Samuel Lockett."

"I pray that they, along with all the soldiers, remain safe there in Vicksburg. My husband told me, just last week, that it looked as though another battle was going to happen there," said Frances.

"You know, that it was almost two years ago when the Stars and Bars flag was first designed and created. As the civil war has progressed, viewed on the battlefield, the new flag was becoming confused and mistaken for the Union flag at first glance, so it was soon retired. The Confederate flag we have today has taken its place," Mary said.

"When have you heard from your son, Samuel?"

"Not for quite a while now. In his last letter to us, Sam told about his unit being placed on stand-by to wait for dispatch orders to Vicksburg. I feel like he may already be there."

"So, Nicola Marschall could also be there as well, do you think so, Mary?"

"That's quite possible, Frances. All we can do is continue to keep them in our prayers."

"Did you hear about what happened at the Johnson house across the street a few days ago?" Frances asked.

"I vaguely remember that Nape may have mentioned something about it, but he rattles on about so much that happens around town, I hardly pay him no mind. Tell me about it, dear."

"You know that William H. is no longer a home guard, but a friend relayed a message to him that a report had been filed at their headquarters about the incident. Late one night, a lone Confederate soldier hid out underneath her back porch, along with his horse. He slept there all night, and was gone early the next morning." Frances said.

"What about Dorothy Johnson and all her children? I wonder if she knew he was lurking at the back of her house?" asked Mary.

"The report stated that she fed him breakfast, and afterward, he left right before sun up."

"She could have been raped or killed right in front of her children!" Mary exclaimed.

"This un-named soldier was an officer, and there was no indication of any personal harm done to her. After she was thoroughly questioned, Mrs. Johnson stated it was her Christian belief and duty to give food and shelter to a man who claimed to have not had anything to eat for three days."

"Dorothy was a lot braver than I would have been," Mary replied.

"Anyway, no harm was done, but it serves as a reminder that Yankees and Confederate deserters could be traveling through our town at any time," Frances said.

"Have you ever been inside of the Johnson house?" Mary asked.

"Last spring, I walked over and we sat on the front porch for a while to visit. Dorothy never invited me to go inside. While her husband, Fred, was still alive, they never seemed to be very cordial or friendly. William, nor I, never became closely acquainted with either of them."

"I remember when the house was first built in 1861. It looked to me like it was going to be quite similar to yours, Frances. I would love to see inside it one of these days,"

Mary said while she offered Frances another cup of tea. "I may just turn out a rum cake next week and march myself right over there!"

"Thank you for having me over for tea. Everything was nice, especially your delicious tea cakes and the visit," said Frances while she stood to leave. Henry, Elizabeth, and the girls are coming to the house for supper this evening. I really need to go now to see that Delce has everything under control."

"Come over, anytime, Frances. I would love a visit since I don't have much longer until I am totally in confinement."

"I wish you well, Mary, and please let us know when you have the baby, now don't forget!"

Mary walked Frances to the side door, and after the two ladies said their goodbyes, Frances made her way across the back lawn and into the kitchen to find Delce.

"Mmm… Delce, something smells wonderful in here," Frances said to her while she stood in the doorway of the kitchen.

"Missus Frances, that's a fresh apple pie I baked this afternoon, and have just put it into your pie safe for desert after supper this evening."

"Well, I'm telling you, Delce, if it tastes as good as it smells, William and Henry are going to be in for a real treat when we cut into this pie. How's the ham coming along?"

"The ham just about done baking. The pole beans are cooking on the stovetop, and when I take out the ham, I'll be putting the yams in the oven. Will you be wanting biscuits or cornbread with the meal?"

"I think the cornbread will do nicely, Delce. When have you heard from Micah and Cassie?"

"I haven't heard from Micah in quite some time, but in his last letter he tells me he is doing fine and likes living in New York very much. He is twenty-four now, and has taken the name of Michael Johnson for his legal name. He shares an apartment with another young man and just calls his name Bradley. He tells me it is a business arrangement between them as partners, and they each split the cost of rent, the electric and heating bills, plus their food. I don't really understand why he chooses to live this way, but I don't believe he could make it there on his own. It would be hard to make enough money while working as a bell hop in a hotel on Fifth Avenue to pay all this himself, don't you think?"

"After he left the Marion Male Academy, I thought he was going to marry the pretty little girl over in Bibb County. What was her name?" Frances asked.

"Her name Viola, and she broke their engagement a long time ago."

"To answer your question, Delce, no, I don't think Micah could afford to live in New York on his own right now. Times are hard enough here, and I can only imagine the cost of living in New York."

"He says Bradley is going to help him get started in theatre; he says he wants to design sets or maybe even do some acting. That boy makes me worry a lot, Missus Huntington."

"Delce, at his age, you're going to have to let him go, it's not worth all the worry. I know you have done your best for him, along with everything William and I have helped with on occasion, but he is now a man on his own. Tell me about Miss Cassie."

"Well, Cassie done changed her name, too, and now she is Cassandra Lee Johnson, soon to be Montgomery. She is twenty-two and engaged to Mr. Clifton Montgomery from Mobile. They met last year when she and her friend, Davita Washington, took a trip down to the Gulf where she met Cliff on the beach. I haven't met him yet, but Cassie tells me that he is as white as a cotton boll. They plan to marry next spring on the beach, and she will live in his house in Mobile. He is an attorney with the law firm of Wilcox, Bailey, Morgan, and Montgomery on Government Street in downtown Mobile. Cassie has promised to bring him here during Christmas where I can meet him. Oh, Lawsy me, to be young again, Missus Frances, Mmm… Mmm… Mmm… !"

Henry and Elizabeth, along with Fannie and Irene, were right on time that evening. Grandpa William always liked to have his supper at half past five, so their timing was perfect, and so was the supper they shared. Delce was on hand to see that everything went well during the meal. After the delicious supper, William and Henry went out on the back porch to sit while Frances and Elizabeth helped Delce and Vangie clear the dining table. The girls went to the boy's old room to play with their dolls.

William sat in his rocker while Henry sat across from his father in a ladderback chair, while they looked out across the back yard at the setting sun.

"The sky looks so beautiful late this evening, don't you think, son."

"Yes, Daddy, it does. It looks as if God just took his brush and painted on this earthly canvas all across the sky as far as you can see with so many vibrant and beautiful colors."

"I like to sit out here sometimes alone while your mama is inside sewing, knitting, or sitting at her dresser, while she pulls out all the letters she kept from David Yarbrough and reads them. I just let her be, after the time I walked in on her and she was upset. I guess we both still need our private time alone."

"That's good, Daddy, 'cause I still miss David, too. But you know, sir, there are many other families in Marion and all over the north and south who have lost a father, son, brother, or husband to this war. Just last week, my friend Charley Davenport, lost two of his brothers at Antietam. He and his folks are just shattered over the loss of George and James. Those boys were just nineteen and twenty-one."

William looked across the porch at his son. "After President Lincoln gave his Emancipation Proclamation, I told Delce and Vangie, I would free them, and this is what they both told me: Delce said, 'free me from what?' and then Vangie said, 'I's too old, besides where I gonna go?' So, now we pay them both wages for housekeeping, cooking, and cleaning, while they are no longer slaves."

"Elizabeth's family had a few slaves at one time, but since we've been married all this time, she has managed quite well in running our house and doing all the work herself. Of course, I help her when I can. She is a lady who seems to enjoy her privacy. I don't believe she could get use to other people in her house all the time."

"The times are changing, whether we all want them to or not. Plantations of two to four hundred acres depended on slave labor to keep them running; and now they are vanishing like the wind with the loss of slave labor. I never thought I'd live to see a day like this. I believe the South is going down in defeat, while Lee's army thinks they cannot be whipped. The South needs to surrender now, and end this war, especially after their failure at Antietam and Vicksburg." William coughed, and spit up some phlegm in his handkerchief.

"You all right, Daddy?"

"Yes, son, I'm fine, just been having a little cough now and then. I don't believe it's anything to be worried about."

"Maybe we should go back into the house. The cool night air seems to be setting in while you continue your little coughing spell."

"Just a few more minutes, son, and then we'll go in. I want to ask you to do something for me, if you possibly could?"

"Certainly, sir, ask me anything."

"William Henry, out of my seven sons, I have been blessed to have you for the longest, and I thank God for that. Every time I go to the cemetery, I see five of my sons in a row under my feet. I know that years from now that we will both join them one day. Your little brother, my first son, died at eleven months old. I buried John Witherspoon in the back yard of our house in Hillsborough. He's under the magnolia tree about forty steps from the porch. When

I die, and you bury me here in the Marion Cemetery, I would like to be placed there with all seven of my sons, and your precious mother, when that day comes. If you could possibly have someone exhume little John's remains, and put him beside me, well, that would be all I could ever hope to ask for. If you can't do that, please don't worry, it is just simply my last request. I'll leave that up to you, my boy, when that time comes. Now, let's go in where I can visit with that pretty wife of yours. Elizabeth is like the daughter I never had. They say that girls are harder to raise than boys, and I would probably have to agree. I watch you both with Fannie and Irene while you love them just like I love you and all my sons. In my sorrow, I am truly blessed."

Evangeline "Vangie" Hollister, who at age twenty-three, became the house servant for Roswell Huntington, and later on for William and Frances in their home in Marion, died peacefully in her sleep on 23 April 1864. She was seventy years old and had served the Huntington family for five decades.

Delce made the startling discovery early Friday morning in her bedroom, after Vangie failed to arrive out in the kitchen where her work usually began each day. Although she had no family of her own, and few friends, she had the love of the Huntington family who would now miss her tremendously.

Over the years, Vangie had aged gracefully while her small-framed, light-skinned body remained almost the same, only just a few pounds heavier. Her jet black hair was now streaked with grey, and her face now showed very little wrinkles. In fact, Vangie appeared in death as a fifty year old. It was determined later that morning, after Dr.

Haywood was summoned, that her death was probably caused by the walking pneumonia. After she went to sleep the night before, her lungs simply filled up with fluid until she was gone.

Later that morning, William took the wagon uptown to the hardware store, and bought enough lumber and nails to finish a nice coffin for her by the day's end. Delce bathed and dressed her in the outfit that Vangie always called her "Sunday" dress. It was a high-collared, long-sleeved, ankle-length dress made of cotton fabric, stitched with fine lace at the neck and sleeves, in Vangie's favorite color of blue.

Delce re-made her bed, where Vangie would lie in state overnight. The next morning, Henry came to the house with three of his friends to help his father place her body into the pine box and carry it to a gravesite that had been chosen on the back of the property. The boys had the grave dug before noon, at which time William, Frances, Delce, Henry, Elizabeth, Fannie, and Irene gathered there on that Sunday afternoon for the burial.

William made a few comments, prayed, and read the scripture verse from James 4:14.

"Whereas ye know not what shall be on the morrow. For what is your life? It is even a vapour, that appeareth for a little time, and then vanishes away." This was the same verse that he read at David Yarbrough's funeral. After another short prayer, the Huntington's returned to the house where Delce had prepared a simple meal. Several times during the rest of the day, William would think about part of the scripture verse, "Well done, thou good and faithful servant." It dawned upon him that over the past several months that

he and Frances had not been to church since their time of bereavement. He promised God that afternoon, he would return to church the very next Sunday. He also remembered what his youngest granddaughter, Irene, had said to him as they were leaving the gravesite that afternoon.

"Life goes on ... Grandpa!"

By the time Christmas arrived, there was more sad news for the Huntington's. Although no one had been seriously ill or even passed away, the news that Delce shared was quite upsetting. Clifton Montgomery arrived from Mobile, and Delce finally got to meet her future son-in-law. Since he was white, it was going to take some getting used to for Delce, but Cassie loved him and he loved her daughter. Following Clifton Montgomery's persuasive offer, Delce accepted not only him, but his invitation to come to Mobile and live with them. Cliff would not take 'no' for an answer, so with all his charisma and charm, she said 'yes'. Delce would be sixty-three on her birthday, and although she was torn about leaving the Huntington's, Delce knew that she needed to move and be close to her daughter. So, her announcement to William and Frances came as a total shock, but the Huntington's thanked her for all her years of service while they wished her well in this new endeavor. Delce left with Cliff and Casssie two days after Christmas, while she looked forward to her new life with them, and the wedding that was set for 4 March 1865 on the beach at Gulf Shores.

It took Frances only two weeks to find herself a new housekeeper and cook, all in one. The girl came highly recommended by Mary Lockett's maid. Verna Mae's friend, who previously worked at the Female Seminary, was now looking for employment. After an interview at the house, Frances hired her on the spot.

Yolanda Queen Jackson was a forty-two year old widow with three grown children: Deidra, Rachel, and Jiminy. Her husband, James, had been dead for nearly three years following complications from a kidney disease. Queenie was a light-skinned Negress with big brown eyes and pearly white teeth. Her radiant smile was infectious. She had a pleasant looking face, pretty but not beautiful. She was of average height and weight. Queenie was dressed neatly for her interview in a long calico dress, with scooped neckline, long-sleeved, and a ruffled hemline. Her long black hair was pulled up under a matching head scarf. She was available to start work immediately, so that pleased Frances very much. Queenie was given Delce's former room and everything that she had left there. It would take a few days to get the new servant familiar with the house set up and the routine that Frances was used to having, and Queenie seemed eager to learn. Frances was praying that she would catch on fast. Breaking in new help could sometimes be quite challenging. Hopefully, this wouldn't be the case in this situation.

At this time, the war had escalated from Gettysburg, Pennsylvania to Fredericksburg to Spotsylvania to Cold Harbor to Petersburg, and finally to Richmond, Virginia. A reference for all the fighting was that both sides simply called it "the war." Later, the United States Government called it the War of the Rebellion. The South officially adopted it as the War Between the States, though this was never heard until after the war. Most of Europe called it the American Civil War, and by this inaccurate title it is usually known.

On the morning of 3 April 1865, remnants of Lee's army retreated westward, leaving both Petersburg and Richmond occupied by Union forces. General Grant then realized that total victory for him was inevitable. The final campaign of the war ended a week later about seventy-five miles away at Appomattox where the once mighty Army of Northern Virginia was surrendered in defeat. Outnumbered, the 28,000 strong were half-starved and cut off from their escape route by Sheridan, so Lee was forced to surrender. General Robert E. Lee met with General Ulysses S. Grant at the McLean House near the Appomattox Court House to sign the official surrender on 9 April 1865. Unknowingly, General Johnston's small army in North Carolina did not formally surrender to General Sherman until 26 April 1865. Thus, "the war" had finally ended.

Perry County and Marion slowly made its comeback while the period of reconstruction began to take place in towns and cities all over the north and south. The war had taken its toll on so many places with death and destruction in most every region. In Marion alone, the bodies and remains of their Confederate dead were being returned home for burial. Other soldiers were not so lucky, since most of them had suffered agonizing deaths and were buried near where they had fallen. There were numerous soldiers that had been wounded severely, missing limbs, or sick with dysentery or other life-threatening illnesses that were trying to make it home. When the survivors arrived back in Perry County, many were taken to the Breckenridge

Military Hospital on the campus of the Marion Military Institute for hospitalization and treatment.

As far as the lives of William and Frances were concerned, they spent the next ten years simply growing old together. William continued working in his shop when he felt like it, while mainly creating and making various pieces for his customers that were special orders. He would sometimes go fishing with Henry on the Cahaba River in the summer and turkey hunting in the Fall. William would always spin fishing tales to his granddaughters about the one that got away. Frances (Fannie) and Irene were growing rapidly into young ladies, so Frances especially enjoyed being with them every chance she got. Along with Queenie, those four were usually cooking and baking, sewing, or just laughing and telling stories. The girls loved hearing Queenie tell them ghost stories that would keep them spellbound for hours.

Amid all the heartaches from their past, William and Frances' strong faith in God kept them going all through their remaining years. During this time, William wrote several poems and verses as a way to express his feelings about life and the love he had for his wife and family. Most of his writings have been lost over the years, but the poem he wrote at the time of their 50th wedding anniversary still remains as part of the legacy he left behind for his family and friends. It reads:

Soliloquy on the 50th Anniversary of His Marriage
By William Huntington (1869)

We've travelled far, my wife and I,
O'er many a weary road;
But, looking back, we gladly see
They've led us towards our God.

On either side, high rocks to climb
To gain a brighter way;
And when, on that, awhile we trod
We saw, He sent the ray!

Then wandering still, in rugged paths
When sunshine seemed afar
Yet we were led by unseen hands –
With Hope, our guiding star.

Sometimes we launched a tiny boat
And watched it floating on;
Till some high point shut out the view;
Then said, "Thy will be done."
Oft little flow'rets charmed our eyes,
And shed sweet perfume round.
But when they left the parent stem,
We still new blessings found.

Now, near the end, my wife and I,
On this same chequered road,
We forward look, and gladly see,
We're nearer still to God!

4. *Huntington Silversmiths 1763 – 1885 p. 77*
   William Johnston Hogan 1977

William Huntington, at the age of eighty-one, made a silver ring for the former governor of North Carolina, William Alexander Graham, during the month of March 1873. The ring was a gift, and was engraved with the names of the illustrious trio of Clay, Calhoun, and Webster. This creation is thought to have been the last piece of silver made by William Huntington.

Also, in 1873, Irene, the twenty-one year old daughter of Elizabeth and William Henry Huntington, married Mr. Charles Brown in Marion. The next year, Irene gave birth on 3 October to a daughter she named Bessie. Sadly, the infant only lived for twenty-two days and died 25 October 1874.

While the Huntington's were in mourning and still dealing with the unexpected loss of their son and daughter-in-law's first grandchild, and William and Frances' great-granddaughter, Bessie Brown, sudden tragedy reared its ugly head and struck once again, even harder this time. William Huntington died suddenly at age eighty-two on 27 October 1874, only two days after little Bessie. William never seemed to complain while staying active as he could most days. His death came swift and sudden, a possible heart attack. Frances was naturally heart-broken for the rest of her days. William's funeral was held in the church that he loved so much, Marion Presbyterian, with burial in the Marion Cemetery.

William Henry, still in grief over the loss of his father,

along with his wife Elizabeth, were shocked once again when they lost their daughter, Irene, at age twenty-two on 19 June 1875 from an undisclosed illness.

Two years later, following a brief illness, Frances Howze Huntington passed away on 9 July 1877, at age seventy-five. In her will, Frances left the house and all her possessions to her granddaughter Fannie and William Henry. Henry arranged a small graveside service for his mother, after which she was interred beside her beloved William. Later that same year in 1877, at age seventy-six, William's sister, Elizabeth Huntington Parish, also died. Henry had his Aunt Elizabeth buried in the Huntington plot, while later providing the granite markers and headstones for her and his mother and father.

It was never known if Henry was able to grant his father's last request or not since he fell into bad health that may have caused him extreme pain and disability. He was no longer able to work in the shop as the last Huntington silversmith. William Henry Huntington died on 10 March 1885 at age sixty-two. The house was later sold to the Woods family where Miss Susan (Sue) McKinney Woods lived for nearly thirty years until she died in 1921.

But, the story doesn't end here. As the present owner and caretaker of Simplicity, this writer has the hope that its future owner one day will love and care for this old house just as much as he does. Long live Simplicity!

Life goes on ...

William Huntington

1834 Age 42

Image used by permission of Daniel Killingsworth

Residence of Susan (Sue) McKinney Woods
for nearly 30 years
Former home of William Henry Huntington
Only photograph known to exist and taken with
Miss Sue Woods on the porch in 1919
Photo origin unknown

William Huntington
1792- 1874
Image used by permission of Daniel Killingsworth

William Henry Huntington
1823 - 1885
Son of William and Frances Huntington
Image used by permission of Daniel Killingsworth

William Huntington Gravesite
Marion Cemetery
2021
Photo courtesy of the author

Simplicity
1834
Huntington-Locke-Hall
House on West Lafayette Street
Marion, Alabama
Photo courtesy of the author

Myrtle Hill 1840
Huntington-Lewis-Hunter
House on West Lafayette Street
Marion, Alabama
Photo courtesy of the author

Lockett-Martin-Nyman
1840
House on West Lafayette Street
Marion, Alabama
Photo courtesy of the author

William & Frances Howze Huntingon
50ᵗʰ Anniversary
9 December 1819 - 1869
Image used by permission of Daniel Killingsworth

Jon & Paula Kirkpatrick Hall
50th Anniversary
30 June 1967 - 2017
Photo courtesy of the author

Jon Howard Hall
Writer of Historical Fiction
Age 60
Birmingham, Alabama
Photo by ACIPCO Photography 2005

Epilogue

It is unknown to say exactly where Roswell Huntington lived at any time during his life in Hillsborough. The 1790 Census lists him living next to his father-in-law, Martin Palmer. It seems possible that Roswell was about to move into town in 1799 when Robert Eaton sold him Lot 91, but that deal may have never happened. Also, there is no record that Roswell sold any farm land before he moved to Alabama with his son William and his family. The house he actually lived in while in Hillsborough probably belonged to Martin Palmer. If this is true, then the Palmer's and the Huntington's were neighbors for almost forty years.

There is documentation from the probated will of Martin Palmer which states that his daughter, Mary and son-in-law, Roswell Huntington owned a slave named Delce and her children. Among the list of slaves that Roswell sold to William Huntington on 17 November 1829, appeared the name of Delce. The date of the will in 1835 helps to establish the death of Mary Palmer Huntington between July 1831 and December 1833, the date of the move to Alabama.

All the names of the other slaves mentioned in this work

were fictionalized and added to define their individual character.

Although not mentioned in the book, the following churches and schools were an important part of Marion during the early years. They are listed as the following:

Siloam Baptist Church was founded on June 4, 1824.

The Marion Presbyterian Church was organized on July 30, 1832.

Marion Female Seminary was established in the spring of 1836.

Marion Methodist Church erected their first church building in 1837.

St. Wilfrid's Episcopal Church was first organized as St. Michael's Parish in 1838, later to become St. Wilfrid's in 1883. The building that had served the congregation since 1849 was destroyed by fire in 1896, and later rebuilt as it stands today.

Madison College, located three miles west of Marion, opened by the end of 1838. It was first known as the Manual Labor Institute of South Alabama.

Hopewell Academy opened in September 1839, and was located three miles west of Madison College.

Marion Male Academy existed in 1839.

The Marion Lyceum was in operation in 1841.

Judson Female College was chartered on January 9, 1841. Listed as one of five all-female colleges in the United States, Judson College closed its doors in 2021.

Howard College was established in November 1841, and opened the doors to its first building on January 3, 1842.

St. Wilfrid's School for Boys was established in 1849.

The Lincoln Normal School was established during the years 1867-1868.

First Congregational Church was built by freed slaves in 1871.

Berean Baptist Church was built by freed slaves in 1873.

Howard, the Baptist College, re-located to Birmingham in 1887, and was later renamed Samford University as it exists today.

The former campus of Howard College was later transferred by a charter granted by the State of Alabama in 1889 to become what is known today as Marion Military Institute. The building that was completed in 1857, and once served as the Breckenridge Army Hospital C.S.A. during the civil war, is now the Chapel for Marion Military Institute – MMI.

Afterword

It has been 188 years since William Huntington left his home in Hillsborough, North Carolina, and traveled south to Alabama to begin a new life with his family in Perry County. With a wife, three small sons, his father, and two sisters, William soon established the home he built, his silversmith and jewelry shop, and some rich farm land in Greensboro.

He had so much to look forward to as a forty-two year old, gifted silversmith, while he lived in Marion for the next forty years. During his time there, while his business and livelihood soon prospered, he also suffered near bankruptcy, felt the effects of the civil war at home, and experienced the deaths of his father, five of his sons, two brothers, and three sisters. Yet, he lived to the ripe old age of eighty-two, with no particular health issues, seemingly until near his death in 1874. William Huntington, as an elder in the Presbyterian Church, left a legacy of Christian servanthood in the love he had for his family and his fellowman. His belief in God provided him with the strong faith that he exemplified in his daily walk in life and how he treated people.

If one could talk with William Huntington today, I

believe he would first share that he was far from perfection, and simply a sinner saved by Grace. He would probably go on to say that he tried to treat his family, friends, and customers, fairly and squarely, while always applying the Golden Rule. After reading all I could find about him, I have to say that I soon developed a great admiration for William Huntington and the entire Huntington family. He was a simple man, who I feel overcame all the bad things that happened to him in life by his simple faith and love of family.

Although many things have changed throughout the years since he first built this house, some things haven't and still remain original. The lot and grounds where the house sits is in the same place. The street in front of the house has changed from the dirt road into pavement, while the landscaping is probably the most dramatic change since the original kitchen and outbuildings are no longer there. There is an existing stone kiln located on the west side of the house that William could have possibly used in his work as a silversmith.

I love living in the house, while walking through the doorways and rooms that were once occupied by the Huntington's where they received family members, friends, and guests in their home. The walls where mirrors and pictures once hung, and the original heart pine floors where they walked, that now have been sanded and stained. I believe the front door to be original to the house, as well as the five mantels and chimneys. The restoration that I have done already and continue to do inside and outside the house, I like to think that the Huntington's would approve if they could see the place now in 2021. It is my hope and concern that events in the future will allow this home to be kept and preserved for as long as it can stand here on West Lafayette Street.

Adding to the Huntington legacy, I would like to end by saying that I would hope the Hall legacy would be similar. I am a simple man who loves God, my Lord Jesus Christ, family, and friends. May the next owner and caretaker love this old house as much as I love it!

9:37 p.m.
October 15, 2021
Marion, Alabama

Huntington Timeline

1737 – Joseph Gale born in Boston, Massachusetts on 1 March

1740 – Ebenezer Huntington born in Norwich, Connecticut on 27 September

1743 – Sarah Edgerton born in Norwich, Connecticut on 20 March

1763 – Roswell Huntington born in Norwich, Connecticut on 15 March

1763 – Roswell Huntington baptized in the First Congregational Church on 22 March

1763 – Ebenezer Huntington dies and is buried in the West Indies before 6 September

1765 – Sarah Edgerton Huntington is married to Joseph Gale in Norwich on 15 June

1765 – Mary Palmer born in Hillsborough, North Carolina

1768 – Sarah Gale, daughter of Joseph and Sarah Gale, born in Norwich, Connecticut

1769 – Captain Daniel Throop appointed legal guardian of Roswell Huntington on 5 April

1770 – Joseph Gale, son of Joseph and Sarah Gale, born in Norwich, Connecticut

1774 – William Huntington (uncle) appointed guardian of Roswell Huntington on 23 Nov.

1776 – William Gale, son of Joseph and Sarah Gale, born in Norwich, Connecticut

1777 – Andrew Huntington (uncle) appointed guardian of Roswell Huntington on 5 August

1779 – Mary Gale, daughter of Joseph and Sarah Gale, born in Norwich, Connecticut

1780 – Mary Gale, daughter of Joseph and Sarah Gale, dies in Norwich (age 1)

1781 – John Gale, son of Joseph and Sarah Gale, born in Norwich, Connecticut

1784 – Roswell Huntington (age 21) becomes apprentice to silversmith Joseph Carpenter

1785 – Polly Gale, daughter of Joseph and Sarah Gale, born in Norwich, Connecticut

1785 – Roswell Huntington moves to Hillsborough, North Carolina

1786 – Roswell Huntington meets Mary (May) Palmer in Hillsborough, North Carolina

1787 – Sarah Edgerton Huntington Gale dies in Norwich, Connecticut (age 44)

1789 – Roswell Huntington married to May Palmer in Hillsborough, North Carolina

1790 – Sarah Huntington, daughter of Roswell and May Huntington born on 11 November

1792 – William Huntington, son of Roswell and May Huntington born on 8 September

1796 – Priscilla Huntington, daughter of Roswell and May Huntington, born in Hillsboro

1797 – Martin Palmer Huntington, son of Roswell Huntington, born in Hillsboro, NC

1799 – Joseph Gale dies in Norwich, Connecticut in December (age 62)

1800 – Nancy Huntington, daughter of Roswell and May Huntington, born in Hillsboro

1801 – Elizabeth Huntington, daughter of Roswell and May Huntington born in Hillsboro

1802 – Frances Robeson Howze born in Franklin County, North Carolina on 28 December

1808 – John Huntington, son of Roswell and May Huntington, born in Hillsboro, NC

1814 – Priscilla Huntington, daughter of Roswell Huntington married to Thomas G. Wallis

1815 – Sarah Huntington, daughter of Roswell Huntington, married to George Clancy

1817 – City of Marion established in Perry County, Alabama

1819 – William Huntington married to Frances Robeson Howze in Hillsboro, NC on 9 Dec.

1821 – John Witherspoon Huntington, 1st son of William Huntington, born in Hillsborough

1821 – John Witherspoon Huntington dies 31 October at 11 months (crib death)

1822 – Martin Palmer Huntington, son of Roswell Huntington, married to Susan Holden

1823 – William Henry Huntington, 2nd son of William Huntington, born on 14 July in NC

1827 – Isaac Howze Huntington, 3rd son of William Huntington, born on 25 April in NC

1831 – Duke Howze Huntington, 4th son of William Huntington, born on 17 January in NC

1831 – Nancy Huntington, daughter of Roswell Huntington, married to William J. Hogan

1831 – Mary (May) Palmer Huntington, wife of Roswell, dies and is buried in NC (age 66)

1833 – John Gale dies in Norwich, Connecticut (age 52)

1833 – Roswell and William Huntington moved to Marion, Alabama, and also

1833 – Widows Sarah H. Clancy & Elizabeth H. Parish, Thomas & Priscilla Wallis

1834 – Simplicity, aka Huntington-Locke-Hall house, built on West Lafayette Street

1835 – Thomas Roswell Huntington, 5th son of Wm Huntington, born in Marion 15 March

1836 – Susan (Sue) McKinney Woods born in Orange County, NC on 29 March

1836 – Roswell Huntington dies in Marion on 8 September (age 73)

1837 – Thomas Roswell Huntington dies in Marion, Alabama on 1 April (age 2)

1837 – Martin Palmer Huntington, 6th son of Wm Huntington, born in Marion on 27 Oct.

1839 – John Huntington, son of Roswell Huntington, married to Salina Gray

1839 – Polly Gale dies in Norwich, Connecticut (age 54)

1840 – David Yarbrough Huntington, 7th son of Wm Huntington, born in Marion 16 Oct.

1844 – Duke Howze Huntington dies in Marion, Alabama on 6 September (age 14)

1850 – Isaac Howze Huntington dies in Marion, Alabama on 12 October (age 23)

1851 – Martin Palmer Huntington, son of Roswell Huntington, dies in Marion (age 54)

1852 – Martin Palmer Huntington, son of Wm Huntington, dies on 28 August (age 15)

1855 – John Huntington, brother of Wm Huntington, dies in Pontotoc, Miss. (age 47)

1856 – Sarah H. Clancy, sister of Wm Huntington, dies on 28 October (age 66)

1858 – Priscilla Huntington Wallis dies in Marion, Alabama (age 62)

1858 – Nancy Huntington Hogan dies in Hillsborough, North Carolina (age 58)

1860 – William Gale dies in Norwich, Connecticut (age 84)

1862 – David Yarbrough Huntington dies in 2nd Battle of Manassas 30 Aug. (age 22)

1874 – William Huntington dies in Marion, Alabama on 27 October (age 82)

1877 – Frances Howze Huntington dies in Marion, Alabama on 9 July (age 75)

1877 – Elizabeth Huntington Parish dies in Marion, Alabama (age 76)

1885 – William Henry Huntington dies in Marion, Alabama on 10 March (age 62)

The Seven Children of Roswell and Mary Palmer Huntington

Sarah (1790-1856) married to George Clancy in 1815

William (1792-1874) married to Frances
Robeson Howze in 1819

Priscilla (1796-1858) married to Thomas G. Wallis in 1814

Martin Palmer (1797-1851) married
to Susan Holden in 1822

Nancy (1800-1856) married to William
Johnston Hogan in 1831

Elizabeth (1801-1877) married to Charles Parish in 1819

John (1808-1855) married to Salina Gray in 1839

The Seven Sons of William and Frances Howze Huntington

JOHN WITHERSPOON HUNTINGTON – b.
1821 in Hillsborough, North Carolina
d. – 31 October 1821 (age 11 mos.) in
Hillsborough, North Carolina

WILLIAM HENRY HUNTINGTON – b. 14
July 1823 in Hillsborough, North Carolina
d. – 10 March 1885 (age 62) in Marion, Alabama

ISAAC HOWZE HUNTINGTON – b. 25 April
1827 in Hillsborough, North Carolina
d. – 12 October 1850 (age 23) in Marion, Alabama

DUKE HOWZE HUNTINGTON – b. 17 January
1831 in Hillsborough, North Carolina
d. – 6 September 1844 (age 14) in Marion, Alabama

THOMAS ROSWELL HUNTINGTON – b.
15 March 1835 in Marion, Alabama
d. – 1 April 1837 (age 2) in Marion, Alabama

MARTIN PALMER HUNTINGTON – b.
27 October 1837 in Marion, Alabama
d. – 28 August 1852 (age 15) in Marion, Alabama

DAVID YARBROUGH HUNTINGTON – b.
16 October 1840 in Marion, Alabama
d. -30 August 1862 (age 22 – killed in
the 2nd Battle of Manassas)
Buried in the Marion Cemetery

St. Wilford's Episcopal Cemetery

From 24 October 1855 – 17 December 1877, the parish records of St. Wilfrid's Episcopal Church states that people of color, both slave and free, were buried in St. Wilfrid's Cemetery.

CONFEDERATE REST
1873 – 1874

During the War Between the States, Breckenridge Military Hospital was established at what is now Marion Military Institute. Soldiers who died were first buried behind the MMI campus. After the war, the Ladies Memorial Association of Montgomery had the remains exhumed and re-interred in St. Wilfrid's Cemetery. A redwood tree from California was planted there as a living memorial to the fallen soldiers by Mrs. Porter King. This section of the cemetery was given the name Confederate Rest.

The men interred there in their final rest include the following list of names in alphabetical order:

Bell, F. N.
Dansmore, W. S.
Fowler, W.
Grier, J.
Harmon, J. J.
Harris, J.
Massey, C. D.
Montgomery, J.
O'Neil, J. W.
Swan, J. A.
Tillerson, C. W.
Williams, N.

87 Unknown

Simplicity 1834

List of Previous Homeowners – 217 West Lafayette Street – Marion, Alabama

1834 – 1836 Roswell Huntington

1836 – 1874 William Huntington

1874 – 1877 Frances Huntington

1877 – 1885 William Henry Huntington

1885 – 1921 Susan (Sue) McKinney Woods

1922 – 1974 Judson Cleveland Locke Sr.

1974 – 2000 Judson Cleveland Locke Jr.

2000 – 2003 Frederick & Trisha Bohlen

2003 – 2004 Alexis B. Barnes

2004 – 2005 Vincent G. Palestro

2005 – 2013 Michael N. Bortnick

2013 – 2019 Marion Bank & Trust

31 October 2019 - Jon Howard Hall

Acknowledgments

A special word of thanks to the staff at iUniverse for their work with me during the entire publishing process. Each individual helped to make this experience run smoothly and effortless.

To my editor, Steve Collins, as always I appreciate your help with all the necessary corrections to allow me to present my manuscript in its best form. Thank you very much.

A very special thanks to my sister-in-law, Gale, photographer and owner of Gale Kirkpatrick Portrait Design, who shot the pictures for the cover and author photographs.

Thank you, Sheila Ferrell of Selma, who designed and created the sign for the house – Huntington-Hall – Simplicity 1834.

I offer my sincere appreciation to the following individuals from Marion who provided me with so much valuable information about the actual history. Thank you so much to Blake Barnes, Kay Beckett, John and Zoe Hunter, Constance Longforth, Karen Nyman, and Ann Rankin Price.

And last, but not least, thank you to all my family, friends, and readers everywhere for your encouragement, love, and support. I am truly blessed!

JON HOWARD HALL

References

Dictionary of North Carolina Biography
Edited by William S. Powell
University of North Carolina Press 1979

Roswell Huntington, article
Mary Claire Engstrom 1988

William Huntington, article
Mary Claire Engstrom 1988

Huntington Silversmiths 1763 – 1885
William Johnston Hogan
Sir Walter Press 1977

Encyclopedia of Alabama
Marion, article
Lauren Wiygul, Auburn University 2009

Encyclopedia of Alabama
Perry County, article
Donna J. Siebenthaler, Auburn University 2007

The Second Battle of Bull Run (Manassas)
Wikipedia Encyclopedia 2021

Perry County
Eleanor C. Drake
Arcadia Publishing 2010
Charleston, South Carolina

Historic Plantations of Alabama's Black Belt
Jennifer Hale
History Press Publishing 2009
Charleston, South Carolina

History of a Free People
Henry W. Bragdon & Samuel P. McCutchen
The Macmillan Company 1964
New York

Perry County Heritage – Vol. I
W. Stewart Harris
Perry County Historical and Preservation Society Press
1991

The Union 1861-1865
"Yankees Through Rebel Eyes"
Essay by Clifford Dowdey
Columbia Records Legacy Collection
1950

Grant and Lee: The Virginia Campaigns 1864-1865
William A. Frassanito
1983

Printed in the United States
by Baker & Taylor Publisher Services